The Bogie in the Boat

You know what doesn't go down well with morning coffee? A body in a canal. But when a neighbor finds a grim discovery in the waterways of Venice Beach, Linx Maxwell gets an unexpected visitor in the form of a new ghost. The only problem? Her new ghost doesn't see eye to eye with her old one.

Detective Frank Bogle doesn't know what to make of the young victim. Haunting Linx is his job, and he doesn't want company. All the same, he can hardly deny that the excitement of an unsolved crime intrigues him. The new ghost claims he was murdered—and the trail leads right to the home of Linx's new client.

Two ghosts? One is bad enough! Linx will do anything to get rid of the unwelcome company, including snooping around a tech millionaire's house, posing as the victim's girlfriend, and catching the attention of the very handsome—and very alive—Detective Lee.

Recurve Press, LLC
PO Box 4034
Visalia, CA 93278
USA

Cover: Damonza
Edited by: Victory Editing
Paperback Edition: July 2018

LINX & BOGIE

The Bogie in the Boat

ELIZABETH HUNTER

Now You See Me

IT WAS Saturday morning at my grandmother's house, and Bogie and I were reading the paper. Or rather, I was trying to read the paper and Bogie was—

"Page," he barked.

I rolled my eyes, reached over, and turned the page of the Sports section. It was the only part of the paper Frank ever wanted to read, but since he was a ghost, he couldn't exactly turn the pages himself. I picked up my mobile phone and added an event to my calendar for the next weekend. The editor had called the exhibit at LACMA "pretentious and unmoving." Maybe it made me "perverse and masochistic," but reviews like that made me want to see it more.

"Page."

"I am not your secretary," I muttered. Then I turned the page anyway. It was easier than listening to him complain.

"If you were my secretary, I'd fire you for having

pink hair." He was wearing a pin-striped navy suit that morning. I'm sure any secretary Detective Frank Bogle'd had in his abbreviated life would have been dressed as snazzily as Frank. Pencil skirt, stylish blouse, and horn-rimmed glasses maybe. A no-nonsense gal for a no-nonsense detective. The thought made me smile.

"What are you smiling about?"

"Did you even have a secretary?"

"The department did. Dora." His slightly transparent form shivered. "She was terrifying but efficient."

"Yeah." I turned the page and skimmed my finger down the upcoming events. "I'd suck at being a secretary." My finger stopped at a mention of the Egyptian Theatre in Hollywood. "Hey! *The Big Heat* is playing next Sunday at the Egyptian."

That pulled his attention away from the football scores. "Really?"

"Yeah, you want to— Ah, shit. Next Sunday is Farah's opening in Santa Monica. We can't go."

Frank gave me a dirty look and looked back at his paper. "Page."

He was pissed off at me, but I couldn't do anything about that. I'd promised Farah when I saw him last week. Unfortunately, Frank wasn't the kind of ghost who could go where he wanted. He was stuck with me.

In truth, most ghosts didn't have that kind of freedom. My grandmother saw spirits who were attached to geography, places that held special meaning for them in life. My mother connected with ghosts who hung around loved ones. Well, usually it was loved ones. Sometimes ghosts hung around hated ones. Those ghosts were a lot less fun.

And I had Frank. Just Frank. He was my bogie, had been since I was thirteen. According to my nan, not one of the Maxwell women had ever been stuck with just one ghost her whole life. I was praying I wasn't going to be the first.

Not that I didn't like Frank. He was practically part of the family at this point. But he could be a little—

"Page!"

I slammed down my paper and gritted my teeth.

"What?" he said. "I've said it three times now."

Just to be contrary, I stood and went to refill my coffee cup. Frank loved coffee almost as much as he loved cigarettes. So partly I wanted more coffee and partly I just wanted to annoy him.

"Seriously?" he said, tapping phantom fingers on the kitchen table. "You're such a little kid sometimes."

"And you're more than a little dead." I refilled my coffee and leaned against the counter. "So guess who gets to decide when your page gets turned. Coffee?" I waved the steaming cup at him.

He fought a smile. "Now you're just being mean."

I heard a tap at the door and figured it was old Mrs. Lamberti from across the street. She was a friend of my nan's and would usually come by on Saturday mornings. I went to the door and opened it just as she was raising her hand to knock again.

"Morning, Mrs. L! Nan's not here—she went to the farmers' market with my mom—but you're welcome to come in for a cup of coffee if you want. She'll probably be back pretty soon."

Mrs. Lamberti went a little pink in the cheeks. "Well, you might be able to help me, Lindsay."

All my friends called me Linx, but my grandmother's friends watched me grow up as a Lindsay, and it seemed rude to correct an eighty-two-year-old woman. "Sure, what's up? Did you need help moving something?"

I'm about five foot two inches and one hundred and thirty pounds soaking wet, but Mrs. Lamberti was even smaller than me. Plus I was strong. I'd climbed plenty of walls and fences when I was a teenager, and I was pretty fit from hauling ladders and paint buckets around.

"Well…" The pink was still there. "It's not moving something. But I know Peggy says you take after her with the… other things." She crossed herself quickly, and I realized she was talking about the "ghost thing."

"Ah," I said. "Gotcha."

My grandmother and my mom didn't make a secret of the fact they saw ghosts; most people just thought they were nuts. But Venice Beach used to be pretty forgiving to eccentrics. These days, not so much. But then, nobody was going to say anything to my nan. My grandmother had lived in this neighborhood longer than anyone except Mrs. Lamberti.

"Why don't you come in for coffee?" I held the door open and ushered her to the kitchen. "Tell me what's up. I might be able to help."

"Well, it was the strangest thing," she started. "You

know my hip bothers me in the mornings, so I usually don't go down to the water until it warms up."

"Uh-huh."

Frank raised an eyebrow when we walked in, any irritation with me long forgotten. He lived for this stuff. He'd been a homicide detective when he was alive. He was constantly dragging me into awkward situations that could get me arrested because they were none of my business. He regularly ignored my objections about that fact. Having something weird show up on our doorstep was probably his version of Christmas.

"So you don't go down to the water in the morning because of your hip," I prompted. "But did you do something different today?"

She sipped the cup of coffee I'd put in front of her. She took it black like my nan. "I did. I just felt like I needed to walk out on the back deck this morning. The idea just wouldn't leave me alone."

Frank stood up. "She's got a ghost. Let's go."

"Will you just calm down?" I said. "Let her talk."

Mrs. Lamberti looked around in alarm. "I'm sorry?"

I waved a hand. "That was just Frank. Go on. So you went out to the back deck?"

Mrs. Lamberti's place was a gorgeous wood-shingled house, and it sat on a quiet corner of the Sherman Canal. It was easily worth a few million dollars these days, but she'd lived there for over fifty years. Mr. Lamberti had been a builder, and he'd set his family up well.

Mrs. Lamberti was still looking around the kitchen

with wide eyes, but she continued. "I went out on the back deck and noticed the plants needed watering."

"Okay…?"

"And when I went down to get the hose, I saw that little boat my grandson keeps on our dock. You know the one?"

"Yep." I couldn't figure out where this was going. I refilled my coffee cup and sat down, prepared to settle in for a nice long ramble with Mrs. L.

"So there was the boat that Camden keeps," she continued, "and it was fine… But there was a dead man in it, so that's what I wanted to talk to you about."

I spit coffee all over the newspaper.

"Hot damn," Frank said. "This weekend just got a lot more interesting."

———

"WHY AREN'T we calling the police again?" I asked as I walked Mrs. Lamberti back to her house, Frank trailing behind me.

"What's that, dear?"

"Nothing, Mrs. L. Let me just get you settled in the kitchen, and I'll take a look in the backyard to see if I can get anything." I glared at Frank. "And then we are definitely calling the police."

"I just want to be sure there isn't anything… odd on the back deck. You understand?"

"Of course."

If the victim had a violent death, it was very likely he'd be hanging around. I'd be able to sense him, but I wouldn't be able to see or talk to him. I could only see and talk to Frank. I'd already called my nan. This kind of stuff was her department.

"We need to take a look at the scene before the police come," Frank said. "Once they're in, it'll be harder to get information. I need to see the body."

"No, you do not," I hissed. "If this guy was murdered—"

"Oh, I don't think it was anything like that," Mrs. Lamberti said. "I didn't see any blood. I think he was one of those sad young people with the drugs."

"Well, we'll check it out anyway."

Frank looked deflated. Drug overdose wasn't nearly as exciting as murder. "It could still be murder."

"The fact that you're hoping it was murder should be disturbing to you, Frank."

Mrs. Lamberti was used to Maxwell women talking to people she couldn't see. Luckily, modern technology had come through for mediums. I grabbed the Blue-tooth earpiece for my phone and stuck it in my ear. That way if I was yelling into thin air, people would just assume I was rude, not crazy.

I crossed the street and opened Mrs. Lamberti's side door—she'd left it unlocked, of course—and started to make coffee. Frank was practically bouncing around the room he was so impatient. But I got the old woman settled with the coffeepot going before I walked toward the french doors leading out to the enormous back deck.

I took a deep breath and walked outside, prepared to feel the itch that told me a spirit was hanging around, but all I felt was Bogie.

"Hey, kid, come over here." He was already standing at the edge of the dock, looking down into the water. "Mrs. L is probably right." He sounded disappointed. "Looks like an overdose."

I wrinkled my nose. "So do I have to come and look?"

"Just get over here, Linx. It's not that bad."

I walked to the edge of the deck and looked down. Sure enough, a young Caucasian man was lying in the bottom of the red rowboat Mrs. Lamberti's grandson used on the canals. The victim had brown hair, and his eyes were closed. His mouth gaped open and his lips were a little blue. He was definitely dead. His skin was pale, and a scatter of freckles stood out on his nose. Something about the freckles made me ridiculously sad.

The boat was deep, so it didn't surprise me no one else had spotted the body. It was early enough that pedestrian traffic hadn't really started up, and few neighbors could have seen the body from their back decks, even if they'd been looking.

"You know…" I cocked my head, looking at the dead guy who was sprawled at an angle. "He doesn't look like an addict."

"Addicts look like everyone, kid."

"You know what I mean." Venice Beach had a lot of homeless people, and drugs were a problem. It wasn't uncommon to find drug paraphernalia on the street. My nan had tried to help several "wanderer friends" over the years with mixed results. My mom claimed that many of the homeless had spirits hanging around them, which was rarely a good thing.

But this guy… didn't look homeless. His clothes were clean. His hair was trimmed. "He looks more like a tech guy than a junkie." Except he had a needle in his arm. That much was pretty obvious.

Frank dissolved and reappeared in the boat next to the body. He couldn't move anything unless he was really, really agitated, but he bent down for a closer look. "He's been here for a few hours," he said. "I'm seeing some bruising on his neck. Fingers maybe?"

"Was he choked?"

"Will you get down here?" he asked. "I can't lift his shirt, and I'm betting there are—"

"Fingerprints. Physical evidence. DNA maybe?" I crossed my arms. "None of which are mine and none of which are going to be mine, Bogie. I'm not touching that body."

"If someone held him down and put the needle in his arm, this is a murder."

"I agree. But you know who's going to have to figure that out? The police. Who we are calling right now." I pulled out my phone. "I don't feel any spirits around here, so—"

"Oh my god," said a voice beside me. "If my mother thinks I overdosed on drugs, she's going to flip out."

I turned with wide eyes to see the dead guy standing on the dock next to me.

And then *I* flipped out.

———

MRS. LAMBERTI'S neighbors bought my explanation for the scream because I called the police and reported the body right after they came running out to their decks. I wasn't screaming about the dead body though. It was the ghost who was sitting next to me on the bench. The ghost whom I could see clear as day. The ghost who was not Bogie.

"Will you calm down?" Frank said. "You're acting like you've never seen a spirit before."

"I see you, Frank. That's it. That's all I see. Why the hell am I seeing this guy?"

The neighbors were looking at my one-sided conversation, so I held my cell phone even as I dropped my voice.

"I'm dead," the ghost kept saying over and over again. "I can't believe I'm dead."

Frank asked, "What do you remember?"

The young man turned to Frank, narrowed his eyes. "You're a cop, aren't you?"

Frank smiled. "And you're a crook."

"What?" I asked. "Why is he a crook?"

"Because only a crook makes a cop that fast. What's your game, kid?"

He hesitated, then said, "I'm a thief. Small stuff. Nothing violent. And I don't remember what happened."

I asked Frank, "Can you really see him? I thought you said other spirits came through with static."

"They usually do." He looked pleased. "I think I can see him and talk to him better because you can see him too."

I put a hand over my face. "This is awful."

"What?" Frank asked. "Why? This is great!"

"No, it is not," I hissed under my breath. "What if he gets stuck to me too? I've already got one of you. I don't want another one."

"Hey," the dead guy said. "I'm not that bad. And I don't do drugs. Can someone tell my mom that, because she's gonna freak out."

I said, "Dude. You're dead. She's going to freak out anyway."

He sighed and his shoulders slumped. "Shit. I can't believe I'm really dead. This is not what I was expecting death to be like."

"Did you ever really think about it?" I asked him.

"Nah." He looked guilty.

"Maybe you can just tell us who killed you," I said. "Then we can… help you to the light or something."

His eyes went wide. "There's a light?"

"There's not always a light," Frank said.

"Well, there ought to be!" I stood and paced the deck. "When is Nan getting here?"

"Miss Maxwell?" A voice spoke from the french doors. "Are you Lindsay Maxwell?"

I turned to see a nicely dressed Asian man walking toward me. He was wearing a serious expression and a suit even though the forecast said it'd be close to eighty-five degrees this afternoon.

"Cop." Frank and the dead guy both spoke at the same time.

If he was a cop, he was the best-looking one I'd run

across. And unfortunately, I'd met more than my share because of Frank.

"Are you Lindsay Maxwell?" the probably-a-cop said. "I'm Detective Lee." He held out a card and I took it.

Why did Frank always have to be right?

2

Too Coincidental to Be a Coincidence

"HEY," I said, trying to ignore the two whispering spirits at my back. I glanced at the cop's card. "Christopher Lee?"

"Yes. Are you Lindsay Maxwell?"

"Like the actor?" I smiled. "Vampire guy? Saruman from *Lord of the Rings*?"

Detective Lee was extra cute when he was annoyed.

"I know who you're talking about," he said. "Are you the Lindsay Maxwell who made the 911 call?"

"Yeah, I'm Lindsay. *Linx*." I shoved his card in my pocket and tried to ignore how cute Detective Lee was when he was irritated. I didn't need to be distracted by that when there was a dead guy in Mrs. Lamberti's boat, a new spirit had shown up, and the dead guy had probably been murdered. "I'm the one who found the body. Well, actually, Mrs. L found it, and she walked across the street to my house. She was looking for my nan—my grandmother—but I was the only one home."

Detective Lee nodded and frowned. "Do you know why she didn't call 911 right away? Why would she call your grandmother? Do you recognize the body? Is it someone she thought you might know?"

"I don't think so." I found that blatant honesty was usually the easiest way to deal with anything relating to my mother or my nan. "Mrs. L probably came over because she thinks my grandmother can see ghosts and she was worried one was hanging around on the back deck. You know, because of the dead guy. Who I don't know."

His expression didn't change much. "I see."

"My name is Vincent," the dead guy was saying behind me. "Vincent Anderson."

I didn't say a thing.

Detective Lee pointed over his shoulder. "Okay. Thanks, uh, Lindsay."

"Linx."

"Right. If you could stay right here, I do have a few more questions, but I'm going to take a look at the scene before the lab guys get here."

"Sounds good."

"Why isn't she telling the cop my name?" Vincent asked as I turned and walked back to the bench on the far side of the deck.

"How would she know your name, dummy?" Frank said. "She tells the cop your name and he's going to suspect she had something to do with your death."

"Oh. That makes sense."

Detective Lee didn't tell me to go inside, so I was just staying put. Part of me was afraid if I left the scene with the extra ghost, I'd be stuck with him. I glanced at my phone. Where was my nan? Where was my mom? I really wanted to talk to either of them, because the new ghost was seriously freaking me out.

Frank didn't let my freak-out keep him from interrogating his first suspect in sixty years. I mean, he'd interrogated people secondhand—through me—but I could tell he was relishing Vincent's presence.

"Give me the story, kid. Let me guess, your memory of the events in question is fuzzy?"

Vincent's eyes went wide. "Yeah. How did you know?"

"'Cause I was murdered too."

Vincent frowned. "I'm so sorry. That's awful."

"You know, it took me a while, but I'm okay with it now."

I slapped a hand to my forehead. "Are you not getting that you are, in fact, dead? I mean, you were murdered. Probably. Are you sure you didn't OD?"

"I've never taken drugs before," Vincent said. "So I don't think I would now. I mean—"

"What's your game, kid?" Frank interrupted him. "You said you're a thief."

Vincent shrugged. "Nothing big-time. My friend and me—"

"What's his name?"

"Her name," Vincent said. "Gabby. Her name's Gabby. Anyway, Gabby's hot, right? Geek girl. She worked at that comic shop on Lincoln for a while. The nerds loved her, right? Hot chick thinks guys who collect comics are cute. So she worked it."

"Comics?" Frank asked. "Like comic books? Those things are worth like a buck or something, aren't they?"

"No," I said. "A first edition or really rare edition could be worth thousands of dollars."

Frank turned to me. "Are you kidding me?"

"Nope."

Vincent shifted. "Yeah, so the geeks like Gabby, and they loved bragging about their collections with this cute girl, right?"

"Ugh." I couldn't stop the sneer. "Did this chick scam guys by flirting with them and then robbing them?"

Vincent looked uncomfortable.

I kept my voice low. "That's gross, Vincent. I'm not saying you deserved to get murdered or anything, but that's super gross and wrong. You probably have an army of pissed-off nerds looking for you. We're never going to find out who killed you."

Frank ignored me. "You said your friend *used* to work there?"

Vincent turned his attention back to Frank. He didn't seem all that remorseful. Jerk.

"Yeah," he said. "New manager moved in and got wise to the fact that a lot of the guys who came in to price comic collections or memorabilia were getting broken into afterward and missing the really good stuff. He couldn't prove it was Gabby, but she could tell he was suspicious. She quit a couple of weeks ago."

"This scam isn't making any sense to me," Frank said. "You guys rob the marks, but then who are you going to sell to? The shops who'd buy that kind of junk would be wise to what got stolen, wouldn't they? Where are you gonna fence useless old comic books?"

"Oh Frank, you sweet lamb." If I could have patted his shoulder, I would have. "The internet, Bogie. You can sell all that stuff online. You can be completely anonymous if you want. If you broke up the collections, I doubt they'd be able to trace anything. With a VPN, they couldn't even track your IP address." I looked at Vincent from the corner of my eye. Yeah, he was squirming. "I'm right, aren't I?"

"It worked," Vincent said. "We've been doing it for a couple of years now, and no one caught on."

I was judging him so hard, and he could tell.

"College is expensive!" he said. "We're not stealing food or... cars or anything. These guys can live without their superheroes."

"The college excuse?" I asked. "Where's your self-respect, dude? You could have learned how to strip like an honest desperate college student." I raised an eyebrow. "You chose poorly."

"Strip clubs?" Frank asked. "Tell me you're joking."

I shrugged. I didn't actually know anyone who'd stripped their way through college, but I was betting Vincent didn't either.

Frank shook his head. "Sometimes I'm really glad I died when I did."

"Miss!" Detective Lee was walking toward me. He did not look pleased. "Who are you talking to?"

I held up my phone. "Me? No one. No one important, I mean. My... grandma. I was calling my grandma so she'd know where I am. And she's a friend of Mrs.—"

"You need to hang up," Detective Lee said. "You don't need to be talking to anyone before I question you."

I frowned. "Am I in trouble? Because if I am—"

"You're not in trouble," he said, clearly aggravated. "But I do need to ask you a few more questions, and I don't want you talking to anyone but me until I do."

I blinked. "How long are we talking about?"

He crossed his arms. They were nice arms. I could tell because the fabric pulled over his biceps, and suddenly I was picturing him in a sleeveless shirt.

It was a nice image.

"Sorry," he said, putting his hands on his hips. "Did you have something more important to take care of than a murder investigation?"

Frank came alive. "How do they know he was murdered? Linx, ask him how—"

"He was murdered?" I rose to my feet. "That's *awful*. I thought it was just an overdose. How could he have been murdered?"

Detective Lee was frowning at me. Or maybe it was just his serious face. It was kind of a frowny serious face.

"Since you're not part of this investigation, you don't need to know that," he said.

"But since I do need to stay for questioning, can you tell me how long it's going to be?" I glanced at the french doors where Mrs. Lamberti was watching us. "Because one, Mrs. L is freaked out. And two, I really need to pee."

Two spots of red marked his cheeks. "You can go to

the restroom. Just stay in the house and don't leave. And don't call anyone."

"Awesome."

"Linx!" Frank almost yelled at me. "You cannot leave that hanging. How does he know the victim was murdered?"

Vincent said, "Dude, I told you I didn't do drugs. Obviously I was murdered."

"Were there signs of force?" Frank continued, following me into the house. "Fingerprints on the syringe? You've got to get more information."

I walked past the shaken Mrs. L because I really did need to pee. I walked down the hall and shut the door, but Frank's head popped through.

"Out!" I whispered. "You know the rules."

"You've got to get more information from that guy. He's into you, even if he doesn't want to be. Make it happen, Linx."

"Out of the bathroom, Frank!"

He disappeared, but I could still hear him and Vincent arguing on the other side of the door.

"So if there's no light, am I just stuck here?"

"I don't know."

"Can we go see my mom?"

"That's up to Linx."

"Do I need to hang out with this girl all the time?"

"You need to shut up now, kid. I'm thinking."

I sat on the toilet and put my head in my hands.

Lord help me, I had two of them.

———

WHEN I CAME out of the bathroom, my nan had arrived. I went to her and let her envelop me in one of those hugs that only my nan can give.

"Nan," I whispered. "I have a new ghost."

She pulled away and her eyes went wide. "What?"

Detective Lee walked in before I could say more.

"I'm Detective Lee," he told my nan. "Are you a friend of Mrs. Lamberti's?"

"I'm her neighbor. And Lindsay's grandmother. Are you the detective investigating this poor boy's death?"

He shot a glare my direction.

"Hey!" I said. "I did tell her that much, but she needed to know why I'd disappeared."

"Of course I did," Nan said. "I would have been frantic if I'd come home and Lindsay wasn't there. Wouldn't your grandmother worry if you weren't where you said you were going to be, Detective?"

"My grandmother? Of course— Wait, we're not talking about my grandmother." He held up his phone. "Ma'am, have you seen this man before?"

I peeked over Nan's shoulder and saw a picture of Vincent looking very pale and very dead. He also looked very young. All the talk about grandmothers got me thinking about his mom. Surely there was a way to let her know what had happened to him.

Damn it. Frank was going to be pissed, but...

I said, "You know... looking at this picture when I'm not totally freaked out, I think I do recognize him."

Frank was in the corner on his feet, glaring at me and making "shut up" motions with his hands.

Detective Lee said, "You know him?"

"Not *know* him. Not really. But I think I've seen him… at that comic shop on Lincoln."

Nan said, "You go to a comic shop, darling?"

"Yeah." I stared into her eyes. "You know I love graphic novels."

Nan caught on immediately. "Oh! Is that where you get them? I thought that shop was only for comic books. Not… graphic novels."

Detective Lee looked between us. "Graphic novels *are* comics."

"Well," I said. "That's a bit of a simplification, isn't it? I'd say… comics could be defined by the serial nature of their story lines as well as the larger fictional world they usually inhabit. And graphic novels are more stand-alone… and can be read like a book."

Detective Lee looked at me like I'd grown a second head. "Right."

"I mean sure, they're related, but it's really a completely different format when you think about it."

"Uh-huh. You said Lincoln Street?" he said, jotting something down in a notebook. "And you're sure you recognize this guy?"

"No." It never paid to be too certain with cops. After all, people forgot stuff all the time, even when they weren't lying through their teeth. "I mean, I think he kinda looks like a guy who I maybe saw there a couple of times, but I can't say for sure."

"Kinda," he muttered, jotting. "Maybe. Can't say." He looked up. "Thanks. That's helpful."

Before I could make a snarky comment I'd probably regret later, one of the uniformed guys cracked the door open. "Detective Lee, I think you need to see this."

I nodded at Frank, who followed the two police officers outside. He couldn't wander far, but he could follow the police out on the deck. Vincent stayed hovering over my shoulder.

"Nan, meet Vincent." I shrugged off the chill that prickled my neck. "Vincent, back up. You're crowding me."

Nan said, "Even I can feel you, dear boy. You really must keep your distance."

"Sorry," Vincent said. "Tell her I'm sorry."

"I will." I thought about what Vincent had told us earlier. "Vincent, if Gabby left the shop a couple of weeks ago, what were you two doing to find marks?"

"Marks?" Nan said. "So this young man was a…?"

"Thief," I murmured, watching the activity outside. They were bringing Vincent's body up now, and I could see passersby being turned away. A few residents paused across the canal, watching and gossiping while their little dogs barked up a storm.

Vincent said, "Gabby and I figured we could still do our thing, you know? We'd just have to be a little smarter about how we found the guys. She started trolling some online threads and message boards and stuff. Then there was this one guy—he was local. Actually just moved to Venice. I think it was even around here. She was chatting him up. Some big tech millionaire or billionaire or something. Really into comics."

Oh, no…

A sinking feeling took over my stomach. "Tech guy who's really into comics?"

"Yeah, he invented some crazy-popular app that was like this online catalogue of every—"

"Every comic ever published and its current market value?"

Vincent nodded. "Yeah! That's it. You know him?"

Damn, damn, damn. This was going to get sticky.

"Yeah, I know him."

It just so happened that Leo Caralt, billionaire tech wonder and new resident of Venice Beach, wanted a manga-inspired mural covering the library wall in his new mansion on Howland Canal, not two blocks from Mrs. L's wood-shingled house.

He wanted one, and he'd seen similar work by a local artist at a coffee shop on Abbot Kinney.

So yeah, I knew Leo Caralt, tech billionaire and current mark of the dead guy talking to me.

I was the artist working for him.

———

"LINDSAY, you cannot go back to that man's house!"

My nan was adamant. Frank was just as adamant.

"This is *great*," he said. "The bruises on Vincent's body don't leave much to the imagination. He was held down and the syringe forced into his arm. Only an idiot was going to determine this was an overdose, and that Detective Lee is no idiot."

Vincent paced and pulled at his ghostly hair. "If Leo

killed me, then we need to warn Gabby. She was the one talking to him."

"Lindsay," Nan parked herself in front of my chair. "Tell me you're going to cancel that job."

"I can't cancel the job," I said. "I'm halfway done with a really big project in Leo's creepy, creepy library, and I have to finish it. Not only would it look unprofessional if I just quit, I really need the money. And the publicity. He has huge parties in that place."

Nan asked, "But why is his library creepy? And why would you go back if this man is a creep? You're not reassuring me!"

"He's not a creep." I shrugged. "Not really. I just think he's kinda weird. And the library is creepy because he has all these action figures. And they're all in boxes lining the walls. Shelves everywhere. I feel like there's all these tiny, imprisoned people watching me all the time while I'm working."

Vincent and Frank both stared.

"I'm with you on that one, kid," Frank said. "That's creepy."

"Super weird," Vincent said.

"But he's not a criminal," I said. "At least, we don't know he is. Clearly he's a suspect, but Vincent doesn't remember who killed him, and we haven't been able to find Gabby. It could be this is a coincidence and Leo is the victim here. Shouldn't we be letting Detective Lee do his job?"

Nan smiled. "He's a handsome one, isn't he? I saw you watching him."

I put my head down on the table. "Not now, Nan."

There wasn't enough coffee in the world…

"If I were murdered, I'd want a dashing detective looking for my killer," Nan said. "It adds such an element of romance and adventure."

"We are sitting with the ghosts of two murder victims. So… kinda not cool."

"I meant no offense to either of your ghosts," Nan said. "What will you do about this new one, love? You have a terrible record of getting stuck with your spirits. No offense, Frank."

"None taken, Peggy." Frank was tapping his fingers on the table, not that we could hear them. It took a lot of energy for him to actually move things in physical space. It could happen, but it was difficult. "What I'm wondering is where the girl is. We need to double down on finding her. Linx, try her phone again."

I sighed and dialed her number, but it went straight to voice mail again. "I've called her six times now. She's not answering."

Vincent said, "I'm really worried about Gabby. What if—"

My mother blew in through the back door. "Hey, guys! Did you hear all the commotion? Police cars everywhere! I swear, it's like an episode of *CSI* or some-thing." She stopped and shivered. "New spirit?"

I exchanged looks with my grandmother. "Weren't you in the marina this morning?"

All the police cars had been gone for a couple of hours. Mrs. L's son had come to take her back to his house for a while. The canals were quiet again.

"Yep. I guess there was some poor girl floating in the

marina this morning," Mom said. "A boat ran over the body and... It was awful. Harbor patrol was everywhere. All the lookie-loos were out. Poor thing."

If it was possible, Vincent looked even paler. Frank looked just as grim.

I had a feeling we weren't going to be looking for Gabby much longer. I picked up my phone and called Raul.

3

It Ain't a Party Unless You Bring the Bolt Cutters

"YOU'RE SICK AND TWISTED."

"But you love me anyway, don't you?"

Raul sipped his coffee and let the steam cloud the horn-rimmed black glasses he'd worn that morning, then scratched the half beard that hadn't been there the day before. My friend didn't have a five-o'clock shadow. It was more like an eleven-a.m. shadow. Raul could grow a full beard in a day. He shaved on his lunch break at the LA County Medical Examiner-Coroner's Office because he couldn't stand the idea of "dead people compounds" being stuck on his face.

Raul was an unusual guy. He was a gorgeous geek. Totally uninterested in women, which didn't stop him from having a fascination with my boobs. He was also one of my best friends.

And if you needed to find out about a corpse in the greater Los Angeles area, he was the best.

"Freak," he said.

"Goth boy."

He lifted the middle finger of his left hand and took another sip of coffee.

"What do you want this time, Linx?"

"You know the body they pulled out of Marina del Rey yesterday?"

He curled his lip. "You do like the messy ones, don't you?"

"Can I get in to see it?"

Raul shook his head. "Not this time. One, it's messy. I mean really messy."

I tried not to notice Vincent's ghost cringing beside me. We were sitting in a café in Chinatown; Raul had agreed to meet me on his lunch break. My burger was mostly untouched on the plate before me. Talking dead bodies usually put my stomach in the wrong mood. Raul, however, dug into his fried-chicken sandwich with relish.

"And two," he continued, "the detective on this one is a hard-ass. A damn cute ass, but he would notice a hair out of place. Stay away from this one, Linx."

A hard-ass, huh? "Would that be Detective Lee?"

Raul lifted one eyebrow. "Do I want to know how you know that?"

"I maybe met him at Mrs. L's house when that body showed up."

Raul raised a hand. "Don't want to know more." He leaned forward. "But seriously, right? He's fine."

"So fine. The arms."

"The *lips*." Raul sighed. "He's all yours. He dated someone in Records last year, and she's definitely a she."

I couldn't *not* ask. "Are they still dating?"

Frank said, "Linx…"

Raul said, "A cop? Linx, he's fine, but he's so not your type. The first time he had to arrest you for trespassing, the magic would be gone." Raul pursed his lips. "Or maybe not. I can see him having a dirty side."

"I haven't been arrested for trespassing since high school." I thought for a second. "Or freshman year of college. At the latest."

Vincent shouted, "Will you shut up about the cop? I want to know about Gabby."

Frank glared at Vincent so I didn't have to. Instead, I took a bite of my burger and waited for Raul's mind to drift back to the dead body.

My bogie understood the score. Most of my life was interrupted by ghost shit. I hadn't asked for it. I didn't really want it. Therefore, sometimes I got to act frivolous about death and murder. That was my right. Bogie got that because he'd been a cop. If I spent all my time with dead people, I got to gossip about cute police detectives with my friend over lunch occasionally.

"So the marina girl." Raul's interest had been piqued. "She's mangled, but she was a cutie. Some geek will be crying in his Cheerios when she doesn't come home."

"Oh? Why a geek?"

"Gabby had tattoos," Vincent said. "Ask him about tattoos."

"Purple hair, manga ink. She had that look, you know?" Raul licked sauce off his fingers. "She was a cosplay hottie for sure."

"I have a friend," I said. "Thinks Marina Girl may be a friend of his, but her mom can't stand him. Won't answer his calls. He's worried about her. What were the tattoos?"

"*Ghost in the Shell*," he said. "Do you know it?"

I shook my head.

"The main character is a cyborg with these plugs on the back of her neck. The tattoos on Marina Girl—"

"Oh God," Vincent groaned. "It's Gabby. It's Gabby."

There was something about hearing a ghost cry that raised the hair on my arms.

"—look like sockets. Like the main character has." Raul shot me a look. "Sound familiar?"

I nodded my head silently, Vincent's cries audible only to me and Frank. "Yeah," I said. "That's her. Her name is Gabby. Don't know her last name."

Raul grimaced. "That sucks."

"Was it murder?"

"I can't say for sure. But if Detective Lee is assigned, probably. You said it's connected to that body at Mrs. L's?"

"I don't know," I lied. "They just showed up the same day. Seems weird."

Raul shrugged. "Life is full of weird, gorgeous. Doesn't mean there's a grand conspiracy or anything."

"Tell that to my nan."

———

I SAT in the car for about twenty minutes after I

finished lunch, waiting for Vincent to speak. His energy had become spiky and dark. It scraped against my skin when he brushed too close. It felt like grief and anger combined. Not a combination I was unfamiliar with, but Frank was better at shielding himself. Feeling Vincent's raw presence made me glad I hadn't eaten too much of that burger. I felt queasy and nervous, like I'd drunk too much coffee on an empty stomach.

"Kid, you need to get it together," Frank said. "This isn't helping your friend."

"If I'm here," Vincent said. "Where's Gabby?"

He was looking at me.

"I don't know," I said. "She might be gone already."

She probably wasn't. If she'd been murdered, she could very well be hanging around, but I had no idea how to find her or where. She could be attached to whoever had killed her. She could be drifting at the bottom of the Marina del Rey. I wasn't going to tell Angry Vincent any of that.

"What else can you tell us about your operation?" Frank asked. "If both of you were murdered, it was because of what you were doing together."

The angry energy spiked harder.

"He's not saying you got her killed," I said. "Just that whatever you were doing—"

"We should go to the storage unit," Vincent said. "Gabby and I were the only ones who knew about it. It's where we kept our stuff until we could sell it."

"Where?" I started the car.

"EZ Storage on North Venice. You know it?"

I backed out of the space in the parking garage. "Padlocks, right?"

"Yeah, but I don't know how we're going to get in. Gabby had the key, and I don't—"

"Don't worry about that part, kid," Frank said. "Linx has you covered."

"She knows how to pick locks?" Vincent said.

Frank said, "Not very well. But it ain't a party unless you bring the bolt cutters."

"Wahoo." I put on my sunglasses as we pulled onto the street. "It's party time."

———

THERE WERE several cars in the parking lot when I strolled into EZ Storage carrying a duffel bag with gloves and bolt cutters inside. No one ever suspected the little girl with pink hair had nefarious intent, so though people remembered me, they tended to view me as innocuous. Which worked to my advantage. I walked with purpose and hoped there was no one in the hallway where Vincent and Gabby's storage room was.

There wasn't. I dropped the duffel bag, pulled on the gloves, and snapped the padlock in under a minute.

Vincent said, "This isn't the first time you've done that, is it?"

"Nope."

I slid the corrugated metal door open, and Frank and Vincent drifted ahead of me as I flicked on the single light and yanked the door closed. Vincent's storage unit was hot, but not overly stuffy. There was no dust hanging in the air and no junk on the floor. If anything, it resembled a library. Metal bookcases lined the walls; they were filled with file boxes, packing material, and padded envelopes. A digital scale sat on top of an old office desk, all the drawers pulled open.

"That's not right." Vincent walked toward the desk. "Someone's been here."

"Gabby had the key?" I walked to the desk and examined the drawers, still wearing my gloves.

"Yeah."

Frank was perusing the shelves. "There're still a lot of comics in these boxes," he said. "You always keep the lids off?"

"No." Vincent walked over to Frank. "Gabby was manic about cleaning and organizing stuff from when she worked in the comic shop. Individual volumes were all in their own sealed sleeve. Boxes were covered. Keep the dust off. Keep the mold out. Protect the merchandise. Some stuff we sold right away. Some stuff she wanted to wait because she thought the price would go up. She was smart, you know?"

"What did she keep in the desk?"

"She had a record book of everything we sold, how much we made, all that stuff. Money was in a safe deposit box at the bank."

"Computer?"

Vincent shook his head. "Paper copy. Some of these guys were hackers. Gabby didn't trust computers."

I left the empty drawers open. There wasn't much to see. It was clear that papers had been removed, but I wasn't going to interfere with the scene more than I had to. I wandered over to the file boxes and flipped through an open one.

"Anything striking you?" I asked Vincent as he looked over my shoulder.

"The good stuff is gone," he said. "Whoever went through it knew their comics. This stuff is mostly trash."

"Why'd you take trash?" Frank asked.

"We took everything," Vincent said. "I was in charge of stealing the collections. I grabbed everything and Gabby sorted it out. She didn't throw anything away though. If something was really common, she just filed it. Every collection has common stuff that's not worth much. Editions with huge print runs, things like that."

"So that's what's left?" I slid the box back, leaving the lid to the side where it had been knocked off.

"Yeah."

I turned in a circle. "Whoever killed you guys knew their comics. Gabby probably told them about the unit. She had the key. They killed you guys and robbed the unit, maybe looking for their own stuff." I turned back to Vincent. "And you kept everything here?"

He looked a little uncomfortable. "Mostly everything."

"What does that mean?"

"There were a few things from a recent job, you know? Not really valuable stuff. Gabby said I could, so I wasn't cheating her or anything. But my dad's a huge baseball fan."

Frank said, "What was the stuff?"

"Baseball cards. It wasn't even what we broke in for, you know? There was this one set hanging on a wall in the dude's hall, and it was from the Cubs, which is my dad's team. His birthday was last week, so I gave it to him. Not really a big deal or anything. That's the only stuff that wasn't here. The baseball stuff."

"What job, Vincent?"

"I told you, the most recent one."

Frank rolled his eyes. "Which was…?"

"The really rich guy, you know?"

"Who?" I asked. "Leo Caralt?"

"Yeah!"

I felt like spitting. "I thought you told me Gabby was just chatting with him."

"Yeah, but he's got a lot of stuff, so I thought we could break in, see how strong his security was. Kind of like a… test break-in. I wanted to know how much time we'd have. If it was easy, we'd go back. And I gotta tell you"—Vincent was looking cocky—"it was a lot easier than I thought."

I rolled my eyes. "Except you got dead, remember, Vincent? Ever think maybe Leo found out it was you who broke in? Maybe his security wasn't as soft as you thought?"

He looked confused. "I guess that's true."

People who think thieves are smart are generally mistaken. Most criminals aren't the brightest. They're just sneaky. There's a difference between sneaky and smart.

"So you broke into Leo's house and what? Took baseball cards?"

"And some other stuff. Gabby was in charge of that. She went into the guy's storage room in back. I just scoped out the rest of the house and saw the cards. Gabby said I could take them because they weren't that valuable."

Frank asked, "Linx, you been back in this guy's storage room?"

I shook my head. "I know the library where I'm working is only part of his collection though. He's got a lot more, but I never asked about it."

I heard something outside. I held up a hand to shut up the arguing ghosts and walked to the door. I cracked it open and listened. The voices were echoing and far away, but I recognized the familiar tenor of LA's finest.

"Shit. We gotta go." I grabbed my purple duffel bag and yanked the door open, leaving the bolt cutters on the floor. They were bought at Home Depot and didn't have my prints on them. They were far less incriminating on the floor of the open storage unit than back in my bag. I pulled the door closed and hung the cut deadbolt in the lock before I took off in the opposite direction of the voices.

These storage places could be mazes unless you knew where you were going, but I'd been in this one before. I walked up and down a few aisles until I managed to find my way out to the parking lot. There were a few other patrons hanging around, watching the cops mill around the front. I could see Detective Lee in the front office, a paper in his hand.

He walked out of the office and into the sun.

Damn, he was just so pretty.

I tried to duck behind the other bystanders before he could see me, but I was too late.

"Miss Maxwell?"

I ignored him and walked to my car, popping open the trunk and throwing in the duffel bag as the crowd in the parking lot muttered behind me. I shut the trunk as I heard him shout my name again.

"Miss Maxwell!"

Frank was scowling. "I swear to the Almighty, Linx. Your hormones…"

I slowly turned. "Hey!" I said brightly. "What's going on?"

Detective Lee crossed his arms and stared at me from behind the mirrored lenses of his sunglasses. Raul was right. His mouth was perfect, especially when it was pursed like that.

He must have caught my perusal, because the bright spots on his cheeks appeared again, and he uncrossed his arms.

"Hi," I said. "Sorry." I could feel myself blushing. "You know you're really handsome, right?"

Apparently Serious Detective Lee could be thrown off his game by a little flattery. Good to know.

"I don't… What are you doing here, Linx?"

"Putting something in my storage unit. What are you doing here?"

He frowned. "Why do you have a storage unit this close to your house?"

"Because it's close to my house?"

He rubbed his forehead. "What?"

I kicked my foot out and scrambled for some kind of explanation. "Uh… because I'm a grown woman who's

living with my mom and grandma. And I need some…
privacy sometimes. For… stuff. You know."

The red spots were back. I thought about what I'd
just told him and barely managed to keep from slapping
my own forehead.

Great. Now cute Detective Lee probably thought I
had some kind of sex dungeon at the EZ Storage on
North Venice Boulevard.

Fabulous.

4

No Surprise Is Good When It
Happens in the Bathroom

"WHAT ARE YOU DOING HERE?" Detective Lee asked. "Really?"

"I told you. I'm putting stuff in my storage unit. I share it with a friend of mine. We both had to move back in with our parents after we got out of school. What's the big deal?" I tried to look concerned. "Does this have to do with the guy this morning?"

"Yeah, you could say that."

"That's awful. My mom said there was another body down at the marina. Is it the same—"

"Linx." He stepped closer and dropped his voice. "I talked to Chuck Morrissey about your family. You know him?"

I nodded. "Yep. He and my nan have been friends for years. I know Officer Morrissey."

"I happen to have a lot of respect for Chuck, which is why I believed him when he told me your family was... eccentric. But that you were some of the good guys."

"Eccentric is..." I laughed a little. "...a very kind word for my family. Thanks for using it."

"I trust Chuck a lot."

He took off his sunglasses and leaned in. I could smell him. He smelled good. Like clean laundry and coffee and mint. When did that become a sexy combination? I didn't know, but I suddenly wished we were back in the storage unit and didn't have an audience or a couple of felonies hanging between us.

"Can you do me a personal favor, Linx?"

Yes! Yes, I can, Detective Sexy. What is your command?

"I... probably can. I mean, what—?"

"Don't be a bad guy, okay?" He waited for my eyes to meet his. "Do me that favor. Don't be the bad guy here."

"I'm not," I said softly. "I promise you, I'm not."

"Good." He straightened. He put on his sunglasses. My suddenly-very-awake libido did not approve of either of these actions.

Lean back. Leeeean back. He was taking the sexy mint and coffee smell away.

"What do you have going on today, Linx?"

He wanted to know my plans? I smiled and had a sudden image of meeting him for coffee when he got off work. He'd be rumpled and tired. I'd be paint-smudged and he would think it was adorable. Was he saying my name more often than was necessary? I hoped so.

Detective Lee was staring at me.

"Oh!" That's right, he'd asked me a question. "Um… Not much. I'll probably go into work later. It's been a weird day, but I need to get back to work." I nodded. "At my job. But I'll be finished—"

"Where do you work?"

"I'm a muralist," I said.

He looked surprised. What was he suspecting? Barista?

Okay, I had been a barista for a while, but not lately. It was a noble and difficult profession.

"A muralist?" he asked. Then he glanced at my hair. "Artist makes sense."

"You're the one who said eccentric, remember?" A thought occurred to me. Detective Lee was used to my rambling now. Perhaps I could ramble with purpose. "I am. I'm an artist. In fact, my current job is right around the corner from Mrs. L's house. Tech guy. Huge comic collection." I noticed Detective Lee's eyes get sharp, and I rambled on. "Leo Caralt. Have you heard of him?" I barely paused. "Anyway, I'm doing a manga-inspired mural for him. Do you know manga?"

Detective Lee frowned. "I'm not Japanese, Linx. My parents are Korean."

I didn't roll my eyes, but it was hard. "Yeah, and clearly the only people who like manga are Japanese people. And big nerds like me."

"I just mean—"

"It's fine. And I get it. Clueless stereotypes, right? Anyway, I'm a huge fan of manga, so it's fun."

"Manga?"

"This job." Maybe he wasn't as bright as he looked. "You know, the mural?" Or maybe I confused him. I was hoping it was the latter. "It's a fun job."

He took out his notebook. "And it's by Mrs. L's house?"

"Yeah, on Howland Canal. Leo Caralt. I have his phone number if you need to confirm it. But maybe mention that you're not arresting me or anything. That probably wouldn't be good for getting a reference."

He jotted down a couple of notes and let out a long breath. "I'm not going to be seeing you at any more crime scenes, am I?"

"I don't think so."

That answer didn't seem to please him. His mouth did that pursed, stuffy thing. Sadly, it just made him look cuter.

"Listen," I said, "you're in my neighborhood. I'm not purposely trying to run into you and make myself look suspicious."

Frank muttered, "And yet you do it so well."

I kept my eyes on Detective Lee, giving him my best wide-eyed innocent look.

"Don't be at any more crime scenes, Linx."

"I'll try not to be." I smiled innocently. "Not that it's not nice to see you. You seem like a... fun guy." I even kept a straight face when I said it.

The corner of his mouth twitched. "Are you messing with me now?"

"Of course not." I put on my shades and walked

around to the driver's side of my car. "You're a very serious police detective."

"That's right." He crossed his arms and watched me.

"Doing very serious things." I opened the door.

"Don't forget it."

I let my smile grow. "I wouldn't dare."

Eventually he smiled too. "See you later, Linx."

"Not me!" I got in my car and started it, rolling down the windows because the sun was baking. "Remember? No more crime scenes for me."

"Goodbye, Linx."

I drove off with a wave. Frank was in the passenger's seat. Vincent was in the back seat.

"Dude," Vincent said. "Were you flirting with the cop?"

"The pool of intelligent men in LA is limited, Vincent. Don't judge me."

I saw Frank nodding. "I like him."

"Of course you do."

————

WORKING at Leo Caralt's house after I'd begun to suspect he was involved in two murders was more than slightly surreal. Same glass-fronted study. Same creepy action figures staring at me from their little clear plastic prisons. Same half-finished wall. Same mysterious tech magnate working in his locked office on the first floor.

Oddly enough, the loud group of workmen in the bathroom was keeping me sane.

Usually all the noise would have bugged me, but today it was comforting. I kept my earpiece in and continued my conversation with Frank. Vincent wandered around the house. I think he was more interested in what the plumbers were doing.

"Just because she was working on him doesn't mean he's involved," I said quietly. There was plenty of noise to cover our conversation, but I didn't want to take a chance. Leo Caralt seemed like the kind of guy who'd watch you from a hidden camera if you were in his house.

"He was being targeted by two accomplished thieves," Frank said. "If he found out, this guy would react. And I don't think he'd call the police."

"Calling them accomplished is a stretch, don't you think?"

"For Vincent? Maybe. For the girl?" Frank paced up and down the library, examining the rows of action figures. "I'm betting this wasn't her first job. She may have fooled Vincent into thinking of her as a damsel, but that storage unit was too organized. She was cool. She had a system. Nothing about this wasn't planned."

"So?"

"So she's scamming Caralt, and she's also scamming Vincent. He's playing one game—let's make a little money on the side with this robbery setup—and she's playing another."

"What's she playing?" I picked up the blood-red paint and began to fill in the outline I'd just drawn.

Frank stopped beside me, hands in his suit pockets, watching as the red eye grew. "I think I like this one."

"That's a first."

"Well, it looks like something for a change."

"Thanks."

I'd agreed on manga inspiration, but it was still my work. A spray-painted mosaic formed the backdrop for the figures I was painting. One, a male, leaned into the corner of the far wall, his long leg seemingly propped up against the edge of the mural, his face literally blank—I hadn't decided how to paint him yet—but pointed at the shapely female figure opposite him. Her hair fell in a long sweep down a naked back. She was looking over her shoulder at the faceless man, her hip cocked in a come-hither pose. She was coquettish and powerful. She stood a little taller than the male figure. Perspective was everything. She was the focus. She was calling the shots. Her arm pointed at the man. Would she be pointing a gun? Or beckoning with a finger?

I hadn't decided on that one either.

"I think this Gabby girl was looking to play Vincent too. Maybe she planned on ducking out after this job. Throw some baseball paraphernalia at Vincent and let him take the fall. Heck, she might have been looking to set Vincent up. Let him be the face of the robbery while she collects on the valuables and disappears."

"He doesn't seem like the brightest bulb in the box." I switched from the red to a seafoam green. "That's for sure."

"Nah, he's a nice enough kid," Frank said. "He just got caught up with the wrong girl."

I lifted an eyebrow at Frank. "Not another femme

fatale." I put on my best Mae West voice. "Say it ain't so, Frankie."

He smirked. "Very funny, kid."

"I try." Just then, the urge I'd been hoping would delay itself ever since I heard the plumbers working came back with a vengeance. "Damn," I muttered. "I really have to pee."

Frank winced. "I don't need to know that stuff."

My bogie could be a bit of a prude about bodily functions. The quickest way to get rid of him was to say I felt nauseated.

I crossed my legs. "Do you think they're almost finished in there?"

He disappeared and then reappeared. "Nope. They still have a rag in the drain pipe."

"I don't know what that means, but I'm going to assume the worst." I eyed the stairs. I knew there had to be a bathroom on the third floor, but I really didn't want to go up there. That was Leo's bedroom, and just the thought of it creeped me out.

But...

"You know," Frank said, "you could use this as an easy excuse for snooping. It's a classic for a reason."

"I really have to pee." I bolted for the stairs.

I'd been given a tour of the first and second floors, which sort of flowed together in an open plan. Lots of high ceilings and loftlike areas. But the third flood—the bedrooms—hadn't been part of the tour. Nonetheless, I was sure a bathroom was up there. I'd heard a toilet flushing a few times.

I walked up the stairs and the lights went on automatically.

Motion sensors noted.

To the left was a heavy set of double doors. I turned right and walked down a hall. Like the first and second floors, the decor here was classic geek. Movie posters and memorabilia up here. A lightsaber that looked like it was used on the actual movie encased in glass. A creature head from some horror movie that would give me nightmares. I opened one door. Closet. I opened the next.

Bingo.

Just like the hallway, the lights flicked on automatically. Unlike the hallway, this decor did not scream geek.

I scanned the room quickly and locked the door, being very grateful I hadn't worn my overalls today as I slid my pants down and sank onto the toilet.

Relief!

Wait... was this toilet seat heated?

Oh no.

I heard a clicking sound, and it gave me just enough time to brace myself. Leo Caralt owned a smart toilet. I did not like smart toilets. I didn't like anything I performed bodily functions on being smarter than me.

A smart toilet—if you've never spent time around people with way too much money—is like a combination toilet and bidet. Which meant when I invaded Leo's bathroom, I not only relieved myself, but I got an unexpected and unwelcome bath and blow-dry in the nether regions.

Not only was it invasive, it was also not time efficient. The bath and blow-dry would take a while. Since I had time to look around, I examined the odd decor that had struck me upon entering.

Most definitely not geek.

Jock chic? Was that a thing? The whole bathroom was stuffed, and I do mean stuffed, with baseball memorabilia. Framed card sets. Bats. Old leather gloves. A lot of it looked valuable and carefully preserved, but the settings were old. Wood-grain mounts and yellowing glue on plexiglass boxes.

Ohhh. Light bulb. This must have been where Vincent had stolen the card set from. In fact, there was a noticeable blank spot on the far wall.

I wondered if Vincent had needed the toilet too.

The smart toilet finally finished its cycle and I stood, pulling up my pants, still taking in the baseball collection.

What a weird room.

It couldn't belong to Leo. Not only did he strike me as the farthest thing possible from a jock, but all Leo's collections were new. He'd never have anything this outdated in his house. Except... he did. But why? It had to be someone else's collection. His dad? An uncle?

Making sure I was fully clothed and my hands were washed, I whispered, "Frank."

I heard his voice before I saw him. "You better be dressed."

"Of course I am." I turned, closed the toilet lid, and noticed the plaque behind me. "Huh."

Frank appeared beside me. "That's more of a wow than a huh, Linx." He leaned in. "Nice."

"What is it?"

The walnut plaque had five spaces, four of them filled. The center one was cracked. They were baseball cards, but they didn't match. Three were in color, one was black and white. Three I saw were Yankees cards, and one was from the Cleveland Indians. I recognized a name.

"Oh hey! Yogi Berra. Cool." I didn't follow baseball, but everyone knew Yogi Berra, right?

"Not just cool," Frank said. "These are five of the most valuable players on the 1961 Yankees, Linx. Roger Maris, Elston Howard, Whitey Ford, and Yogi Berra. That team won the World Series that year. In fact…" He tapped the center mount. The cracked one. "That was the year Mickey Mantle and Roger Maris competed to beat Babe Ruth's home run record. Maris did it, but everyone still remembers Mantle."

"So why the blank space in the middle?" I whispered.

I heard steps on the stairs. Shit. We had to hurry. Unfortunately, getting Frank to hurry when he talked about baseball was difficult.

"I'm betting that this space right here was where old Mickey was," Frank said with a nod. "If you were going to steal one card from this collection, that'd be the one."

"Why?"

"These are all rookie cards, Linx. A Mickey Mantle rookie card in good condition would go for hundreds of thousands of dollars these days. Maybe more."

"Are you kidding me?"

"Vincent mentioned some Cubs cards. Not that

valuable, he said, right?" Frank raised an eyebrow. "Didn't mention the Mantle."

I couldn't wait any longer. I had to open the door. I fixed my expression to wide-eyed innocence again.

"Hi!"

As I'd expected, Leo Caralt was waiting on the other side of the door. He was leaning against the wall, watching me with blank eyes. He was a pale-skinned man around my age with dark brown hair I suspected he dyed. His beard, when I saw any hint of stubble, was bright red. He was medium height. Medium build, leaning toward thin. He wore glasses sometimes, but I wondered if those were an affectation too.

"What are you doing up here?" he asked.

From the look on his face, I was not welcome.

"I'm sorry." I tried shutting off the light, but I ended up just waving my hand in front of the motion sensor. "Sorry. The guys were working on the one downstairs and I didn't want to bother you in your office—"

"So you thought you'd invade my personal space?"

I felt the blood drain from my face. "I'm really sorry. I didn't mean—"

He laughed, and the sound chilled me. His face went from cold to utterly, deliberately jovial. The transformation was so fast I wondered if I'd imagined it.

No, the memory of his blank stare was too vivid.

"It's fine, Linx. I'm just sorry about the inconvenience. Don't worry, the plumbers will be finished by tomorrow. They're installing the new toilet on the second floor. It was the last to be updated."

"Oh. That's great." I tried to walk around him, but

Leo Caralt was oddly hard to slip past. He stepped in front of me.

"Is there someone else in the bathroom?"

"No." I really wanted to get out of this hallway. I'd thought Leo was kinda creepy before, but his sudden mood switch was pinging all my instincts.

"I don't like this guy," Frank said. "I really don't like him."

"There's no one in there?" Leo asked again, glancing over my shoulder.

"No." What was he on about?

"So… were you talking to yourself?"

"Oh!" I let out a little laugh and lifted my phone. "Just on the phone with a friend."

"While you were in the bathroom?"

"Yeah." I managed to get around him. "You don't call people while you're on the toilet? Best time to talk."

Without a backward glance, I ducked around Leo, walked down the stairs, and went back to the library.

"You're right," Frank said as I picked up a brush. "That guy is a creep. You need to get out of here."

"The plumbers are still here," I said under my breath. "I hardly think anything is going to happen with three big guys hanging around."

"Yeah, but you heard Leo," he said. "They're gone tomorrow."

They would be. And that thought chilled me. I still had at least a week left on the mural I was painting. I had a good reputation in Venice, but bad word of mouth could end that quickly. I needed to finish this job.

"No evidence," I said, dipping my brush and getting

back to work. "We're guessing, Frank. None of this means—"

"This Leo guy killed Vincent and Gabby?" Frank said. "Tell yourself that if it makes you feel better. But I'm glad you mentioned his name to Detective Lee, kid. Me personally? I got more questions today than answers."

5

Lying Liars Who... Okay, I Was the Only Liar

"TELL me what we're doing again." I brushed my hair out of my eyes. "And why I'm the one who has to…" I eyed my companions.

Vincent the Thief, a ghost.

Frank the Detective. Also a ghost.

Raul, the tall, gorgeous lab tech. Not a ghost, but definitely male.

All three of them looked back at me, the only female. The only other person, from Raul's perspective.

"Never mind," I muttered.

"You tell *me* what we're doing," Raul said. "We're going to see this guy's mom, and you're telling her you were his girlfriend so you can look at his room?" He frowned at me. "Linx, even for you, this is weird. And kind of cruel. She's grieving. Does this have something to do with your friend who knew Marina Girl?"

"Kinda… I think…" I was flailing. This wasn't my

idea. It was Frank's. "Listen, you don't have to come with me."

"Yes, he does," Frank said. "Grieving people do unexpected things. You need to have someone with you."

Vincent said, "Hey. That's my mom you're talking about."

"And she just lost her son," Frank said.

"Fine." I could tell Vincent was nervous. He was even paler than usual, and his presence felt strange and scattered.

"I'm coming with you," Raul said. "People who are grieving can get weird. Violent even. You wouldn't believe some of the shit I've seen."

"Oh, I think I would." I started across the quiet, palm-lined street, Frank and Vincent flanking me. "I have a high tolerance for weirdness."

The small house was tidy. That was the first and last word that came to mind. It had a postage-stamp yard and blue-painted shutters. Flowers grew in beds that lined the front walk, and the grass looked like it had been trimmed with a laser.

"Nice," Frank said.

I ignored him even though I had a vision of Vincent's mom at this point, and she looked a lot like June Cleaver.

"His dad is a baseball fan," I said to Raul. "Vincent may have… appropriated some stuff for his dad that wasn't exactly legal."

Raul scrunched up his face. "That's… sweet?"

"Thank you," Vincent said. "I thought he'd appreciate it. His birthday is next month."

I said, "It's not *sweet*. It's stealing. He also stole a Yankees card worth a lot of money."

Vincent whispered, "I didn't tell you about the Mantle card."

Frank said, "You think we weren't going to notice a missing Mantle, kid?"

"Do you know how much those things are worth?" Vincent hissed.

I knocked on the door and tried to focus on appearing sad and not annoyed with the ghosts behind me. Raul stood at my side, his hands in his pockets. I heard movement. The lock turned.

I didn't have to fake the tears that came to my eyes. The woman who answered the door was wrecked.

"Can I help you?" Her voice was hoarse. "I'm sorry, if you're here to sell something, it's not a good—"

"I was a friend of Vincent's," I broke in. "I'm so sorry."

I was. I was horribly sorry. Intruding on her—even to help solve her son's murder—was cruel and intrusive and awful. I hated bothering her, but I was relieved when her face softened.

"Oh," she said. Fresh tears filled her eyes. "I'm Vincent's mom, Beverly."

Vincent had turned into a mute behind me.

"It's nice to meet you, Beverly. Vincent talked about you a lot."

She blinked. "He did?"

"Yeah." I heard sniffing and suspected it was Vincent. "I'm so sorry to bother you."

She opened the door wider. "No, it's fine. I'm glad you came. What was your name? Are you... Gabrielle? He mentioned a Gabby a couple of times. Are you Gabby?"

"No, but I knew her. I'm..." I didn't want to say Linx. "I'm Lindsay. I was Vincent's..."

"Girlfriend," Frank said. "Say it. You'll be in immediately."

"I was Vincent's girlfriend," I said quickly. "Kind of."

Beverly's mouth dropped open. "His... I didn't know." She flung out her arms and embraced me. "Oh, Lindsay. I'm so glad you came. I didn't know Vincent was seeing anyone. He was so rarely here, and he's never really told his dad or me... Well, I'm just so glad you're here." Her breath hitched. "This is all so surreal."

I was an awful person. I was also the only link she had to her dead child at this point. I hugged her back. "I'm so sorry, Beverly."

"Please call me Bev."

"We hadn't been dating very long, but..." What did you say to a grieving mother? "He was special. Vincent was special."

"He was." She pulled back and wiped her eyes, nodding silently. "Come in. Please. I'd love to sit and talk a little."

I motioned to Raul. "This is my friend Raul. He didn't know Vincent, he just came for moral support."

Raul—always the gentleman—said, "I'm so sorry about your son. I hope we're not bothering you."

"No, no." She sniffed. "The police… they were here yesterday. And then they called again this morning and had more questions. Bud, Vincent's dad, he went to the station, so I'm here by myself. It was just the three of us, you know? I have a sister, but she's in Minneapolis. She's flying out this afternoon, but this is just… It's just—"

"Surreal," I said.

"Yes." She sat on the midcentury sofa in the neat living room.

Once past the initial emotional explosion, I realized Vincent's mom was definitely not June Cleaver. Her hair was cut in an asymmetrical bob, and though she was wearing yoga pants and a tunic that morning, I saw a woman's suit jacket thrown over an armchair.

"Bud works from home," she said. "He's a financial analyst. I was at the hospital when they called yesterday."

Vincent said, "She's a doctor. A gynecologist."

"I came home," Beverly said, "and the world blew up in my face."

"Vincent told me you were a doctor," I said.

She reached for a tissue. "I just can't believe what they told us. Vincent would never have taken drugs. If there was one thing I told him from a young age, it was how dangerous narcotics are. And I know most moms would probably say that, but I knew my kid, you know? I *knew* him. There was something he'd been hiding lately, but I don't think it was drugs." She looked up at me with narrowed eyes. "Did you ever—"

"Never," I said quickly. "I agree. It doesn't make sense. I never saw Vincent using anything like that."

"I smoked a little pot," he said. "I didn't even like that much."

Beverly said, "I doubt Vincent would even know where to get drugs if he wanted them."

I did, but only because I knew a lot of borderline personality artists who self-medicated. I decided not to bring that up with Beverly.

Beverly asked, "Did the police call you?"

"No. I heard from a mutual friend. He had a class with Vincent and heard rumors he was missing. I asked around, but nobody seemed to know anything. I couldn't get through to him on his phone. Then I saw the paper this morning..." The murder had been briefly mentioned in the paper, but with very few details. There was, however, a photograph of Vincent. It was enough to be plausible.

Beverly nodded. "I'm sorry you had to hear that way. If I'd known your name—"

"It's fine! Vincent sent me his address not long ago, so I decided to come here." My heart dropped. She was a mom. She wasn't my mom, but I was still heartbroken for her. "I'm so sorry."

"You lost him too." She patted my hand. "Someone from school said he was missing?"

I nodded.

Beverly slumped back on the sofa. "I just don't understand any of this."

Raul stood. "Do you mind if I use the restroom, Dr. Anderson?"

"Of course not." She pointed down the hall. "It's the first door on the left."

Frank said, "I'm betting the police are telling your dad right now that you were murdered, kid."

"Is that supposed to be comforting?" Vincent whispered.

"At least they won't think you did drugs."

I had to keep talking to distract myself from the whispering ghosts behind me. "What did the police say?"

"They asked a lot of questions. Where he worked. Where he hung out." She sighed. "He stayed with friends a lot, so he wasn't always here." She laughed a little. "I'm realizing now he was probably staying with you, wasn't he?"

I blushed. "Not really. I live with my mom, so—"

"They looked in his room, but I don't think they took anything. Does that seem weird? If it was a drug overdose, why would they want to look in his room? For drugs?"

I shrugged. "Maybe."

Vincent said, "They wouldn't find the baseball cards. Not unless they tore my room apart."

I was trying to figure out how I could also get a look in Vincent's room without seeming weird. "Beverly, is there anything I can do?"

Her eyes went wide. "You're so sweet to offer. I don't think so. I'd love your phone number though. Do you… Would that be okay? I don't know what we're doing about a funeral yet." Her eyes filled with tears. So did mine. "But as soon as I know, I'll call. If you could help call some of his friends, maybe? I don't know his friends from school."

"I hardly had any friends at school," Vincent said bleakly. "Ask for my Paramore hoodie."

"What?" I asked.

Beverly said, "I'm sorry. You don't have to, but you asked what you could do to help, and I'm assuming you know more of his friends—"

"Sorry!" I broke in. "Of course. I'd be happy to. I'll put a list together and… Yeah, I'd be happy to."

"Ask for my Paramore hoodie," Vincent said quietly. "The black one. Tell her we met at the concert last year."

I didn't want Vincent's Paramore hoodie. It was part of his history. It was part of him.

Frank said, "Ask, Linx. A mom is going to understand that kind of thing."

I began, "Do you think…"

Raul came back while I was talking, but he paused in the doorway, watching me with wide eyes.

"I don't want to take anything important," I said. "But do you think I might be able to…"

Beverly cocked her head. "Was there something of Vincent's you wanted?"

At least she didn't look offended.

"His Paramore hoodie," I said. "The black one. We… we met at the concert last year."

Her face went soft. "Of course." She sniffed. "He has so many sweatshirts, but you can look if you want." She waved toward the hall again. "Please." She stood. "I'm going to make some tea. Do you want some tea?"

No, I wanted to escape, but that would be a shitty thing to do. Raul was nodding vigorously.

"I'd love some tea," I said.

Raul said, "I'll help, Dr. Anderson."

"Thank you," she said.

They disappeared into the kitchen while I rose and walked toward the hall. I could see evidence of Vincent everywhere. Family pictures. A baseball team picture. Pictures of Vincent with a ruddy-faced man beside him. A high school diploma. One of those little pressed hand-prints in clay hanging on the wall.

I felt sad. Guilty for lying to Beverly.

And really, really angry.

Vincent had done a dumb thing, but he'd been Beverly's only son. He'd been a part of this family. He'd been loved.

"I won't ever tell her," I whispered as I pushed open the door at the end of the hall. "Unless I have to, I'll never tell her we weren't a couple, Vincent."

Vincent was sitting on the end of his bed when I walked in, looking far younger than he had before. "Thanks."

I would let her think I had loved Vincent too. Let her believe she wasn't the only one heartbroken over his death.

I kept my voice low. "Where's the hoodie?"

"Bottom drawer in the closet."

I opened the closet and pulled open the bottom drawer. There were about four black hoodies in there, but I grabbed the one with the familiar logo with three white bars. All at once, the smell of Vincent hit me. I was in his closet, surrounded by his stuff. There was cologne and a little sweat. Soap and salt and leather. He wasn't a ghost anymore. He was a real person, and he was dead.

The tears came hot and fast. I clutched the hoodie to my chest and felt his loss like a punch to the gut. Backing out of the closet, I sat next to Vincent on the bed.

"Linx?"

I saw Frank watching from the corner, his eyes narrowed on Vincent.

"You shouldn't have been so stupid," I said quietly. "Why would you do this to your mom and dad?"

"I'm sorry," Vincent whispered. "I'm so sorry. I was just trying—"

"You were trying to make things easy," I said. "You were trying to cheat. Don't you know life isn't easy? Nothing worth anything is easy."

"I know," he said. "I'm sorry."

I slammed the hoodie down on the bed. "Not as sorry as your family." I wiped my eyes. "Where are the cards?"

"Back in the closet."

I sighed, but I went back in the closet.

"Pull up the corner of the carpet," Vincent said. "There's a safe set into the floor."

I pulled up the carpet.

"You have to pull up the carpet pad too."

I pulled up the pad, and it was just like he'd said. There was an old safe set into the floor. It had a combination lock. "Your parents don't know about this?"

"I found it when I was a kid. The combination was taped to the front. The old owners must have put it in. There was nothing in it, but it's set into the concrete, so they couldn't take it out."

"What's the combination?"

"Sixteen, five, forty-three."

I spun the lock open and there it was. It was a shield-shaped plaque with four Cubs baseball cards on it. I didn't recognize any of the cards, but the shield looked exactly like the wood-grained mounting of the cards in Leo Caralt's weird bathroom.

"Look on the back," Vincent said.

Flipping the plaque over, I saw the Mickey Mantle card taped to the back. It was in a plain plastic sleeve, and it was smaller than a normal baseball card. I felt Bogie hovering over my shoulder.

"Wow," he said.

"Holy shit." I didn't need to know anything about baseball to know that card was valuable. It had been perfectly preserved. More, it looked like it might have been signed.

"Is that a signed card?" Frank asked. "Did Caralt actually have a signed Mantle rookie card? No wonder he killed them!"

"Hey!"

Frank said, "I'm not saying it was right; just under-standable from a criminal's point of view."

I ignored their bickering and put everything back in the safe before I closed the door.

"What are you doing?" Vincent asked.

"The police need to find this stuff here," I said as I

spun the lock and put the carpet back, scattering Vincent's tennis shoes over the corner. "This ties you to Caralt."

"But…" His eyes were wide. "My parents."

"Your parents have to know that you stole this stuff," I said. "It's gonna come out, Vincent. If it doesn't, there's no motive. If it doesn't, Caralt gets away with murdering you and Gabby." I walked out of the closet and closed the door just as Beverly and Raul walked in.

"Did you find it?" she asked.

I walked over and picked up the Paramore hoodie off the bed. "Yeah. Are you sure you don't mind?"

She shook her head. "Please take it. I don't know… I mean. All his things." She blinked hard. "Come on out to the kitchen. Raul and I made tea."

———

WE DRANK tea and chatted with Beverly for an hour. She told us stories about Vincent as a child, and I filled in with anecdotes Vincent whispered in my ear. I could tell Raul was utterly confused, but he didn't give anything away. Probably more for Beverly's sake than my own; I could tell he liked her. I did too. By the end of the visit, I was even more determined to see Leo Caralt behind bars.

She walked us out to my car and hugged both of us before we drove away.

"I'll call as soon as I know what we're doing about a memorial," she said. "I really appreciate your helping with his friends."

I nodded. "I'll try to get ahold of everyone I can think of."

"Thanks."

We got in the car and drove away. Vincent and Frank hovered in the back. Raul waited until we turned onto Lincoln.

"What the sweet hell is going on, Linx? Do not tell me you didn't know this guy. The stories you were telling his mom were not made up. The Paramore hoodie? The story about the surfing trip? You knew this guy. Why did you lie to me? Why haven't you ever mentioned him before? You know I never ask you questions, but *what the hell?*"

I sighed and glanced over my shoulder. Frank shrugged.

"It's Raul," he said. "Up to you."

Raul said, "I'm waiting."

"You know how my grandma and my mom can see ghosts?"

He cursed in French. "Don't tell me you're trying to pull that bullshit on me."

"Do you really think my grandma—*my grandmother*—is full of shit?" I glared at him. "Really, Raul? I know you're a scientist, but of all the years you've known her, do you really think my nan—"

"Fine!" He was silent. Angry. "So you can see ghosts too?"

"Yes."

"For how long?"

"Since I was about thirteen or so."

He was quiet for a long time. "And now you're seeing this Vincent guy?"

"He attached himself to me when I found his body behind Mrs. L's house. I'm trying to figure out what happened to him so he'll leave me alone."

I could tell he didn't believe me. Or he didn't want to believe me, but he kind of had to. His mind was probably churning with all the weird shit I'd asked him to do over the years. On the one hand, finally telling one of my best friends in the world was a relief. On the other hand, it was terrifying. What if this was one step too far? What if belief was one favor he couldn't grant? Raul had defended me against "ghost girl" attacks all through high school, all the while assuring me he never believed the assholes who taunted me.

And now I'd told him the assholes were right.

Raul didn't say anything the rest of the way home. He dropped me off in front of my house and drove away. I stood on the sidewalk with Vincent and Frank, wondering what I was going to do if he never talked to me again.

6

Come Hither or Stay Away?

IT ONLY TOOK Detective Lee until eight thirty the next morning to bang on my door.

"Oh, you're the handsome one who's investigating that poor boy's death," I heard my nan say.

"Ma'am, is your granddaughter home?"

"Of course she is."

Wonderful.

I'd texted Raul that morning with no luck. He was probably already at work, and I was due back at Leo Caralt's place by ten. I sat at the kitchen table, sucking down coffee in my pj's while Detective Lee followed my grandmother back to the kitchen. I looked like shit and I didn't care. I stared at the newspaper and didn't look up when Detective Lee sat across from me. My grandmother handed Detective Lee a cup of coffee and then excused herself.

"What's going on, Linx?"

I didn't even look up. I didn't want to be confronted with his handsomeness that morning. *What was his cologne?* No one should smell that amazing first thing in the morning.

"Linx?"

I was pretty sure I'd just lost my best friend. Not even Detective Lee drinking coffee across from me was going to make that better. Even Frank had decided to leave me alone that morning, no doubt sensing my foul mood.

"Linx, why were you at Vincent's house yesterday? Why does his mom think you were his girlfriend?"

I sipped my coffee. It was currently the perfect temperature. Coffee stays at the absolute perfect temperature for a matter of minutes. I didn't want to waste those minutes talking to a cop.

"Linx, don't make me arrest you."

A little voice inside me whispered Raul's words: *What the hell?*

What the hell, indeed.

I sipped my coffee. Still the perfect temperature. "Did you tell Vincent's mom I wasn't his girlfriend?"

"Not yet."

"Good. I think he'd rather you didn't."

Detective Lee was very quiet. How surprising.

"I met his ghost behind Mrs. L's house." I sipped my coffee. Past perfect, but still warm. "He told me he didn't do drugs. I was skeptical at first—there's no rule that ghosts can't lie—but I'm pretty sure he was telling the truth. I'm pretty sure he was murdered."

"Did Vincent's ghost tell you who murdered him?" Detective Lee was using his calm "I'm probably talking to a crazy person" voice.

"Nope." I continued flipping through the paper. "That's not the way it works most of the time. A lot of memories close to death can be very muddled. I've heard the same thing happens in car accidents."

Which was true. I'd read an article about short-term memory and traumatic events for a psychology class.

"Right," he said. "Okay."

I didn't say anything else. My coffee was definitely getting cold though, and I wished Detective Lee would leave so I could refill my mug without him having to see my ugly I-just-lost-my-best-friend pajama pants.

"Anything else?" I asked him, finally looking up.

He was staring at me, and I couldn't read his expression. It wasn't derision, but it wasn't belief either. Detective Lee had a good poker face. He might even be able to beat my mom if he had a lucky night.

"Stay away from Beverly Anderson," he said.

I shrugged. I didn't want to tell him I would because I'd already offered to help Vincent's mom by contacting his friends when the memorial was planned.

That reminded me, I needed to get a list from Vincent before he drifted off to the ether. Which would hopefully be soon.

"We have a line of inquiry, and it has nothing to do with you," Detective Lee said. "So don't be interesting, Linx."

"I'll see what I can do." I looked back down at the

paper and willed him to leave. Which he did a few minutes later. He didn't even say goodbye. I glanced at his abandoned coffee and reached across the table for the still-full mug.

Perfect drinking temperature. At least something was going right that morning.

Frank drifted in a few minutes later while I was drinking the detective's coffee.

"Raul will come back," he said.

"How do you know?" I was perversely angry at Bogie. I knew it wasn't Frank's fault that I'd hidden things from Raul, but dammit, if Frank had never appeared to me, I wouldn't have had to. I would have lived a normal life. Or as normal as could be expected in my family.

"I've known that kid as long as you have," Frank said. "He's not the kind to drop you. He's loyal. And I can promise you that he's wondered about all your weird stuff over the years. Right now he's just pissed you waited so long to tell him."

"Uh-huh."

Maybe that was true. Maybe Bogie was right and Raul would call me back and we'd laugh about this and he'd tell me he was relieved I was a ghost-seeing amateur detective instead of a troubled woman with an unhealthy obsession over cold murder cases.

Maybe.

Or maybe he'd never speak to me again because I was a liar.

"Okay." Frank waved hand in front of my face.

"Time to stop moping, kid. You're headed to the creep's house this morning. Has Vincent made an appearance yet?"

I shook my head.

"No matter." Frank was acting like my gran. "Get up. Get dressed. Caralt is suspicious of you at this point, so the sooner you can get in and out of there, the better. Try to finish up this painting while the workmen are still there."

"It doesn't work that way," I griped. "And I've got another week of painting. At least a week. I can't escape this guy that easy. I'm just praying that he's lost interest or doesn't consider me a threat."

"You keep your phone on and your earbud in at all times, Linx."

"I will." I stood and put my coffee cup in the sink. "Now see if you can find Vincent. I'm not waiting on you two."

———

LEO CARALT'S house was only a few blocks from my own. When I'd taken the job, it seemed like a bonus. Now, passing the dock where Vincent's body had been found floating, with his ghost following me, it felt more ominous than convenient.

Frank and Vincent were chatting.

"Did Gabby know you'd taken them?"

"She knew about the Cubs cards. Not the Mantle."

"What were you thinking, you idiot?"

"I was thinking... I don't know. I just thought... This card is here. And this guy is a total geek. He probably got this collection from his dad or something and he has no idea what it is. He's obsessed with his comic books and all that shit and he won't even notice."

"Anyone as smart as Caralt is going to notice a card worth several hundred grand if it goes missing."

"But he kept it in the bathroom!" Vincent said. "The *bathroom*! Who keeps a signed Mickey Mantle rookie card in the bathroom?"

"I can't disagree with you," Frank said. "But you're still an idiot."

I muttered, "I hear the bathroom is a popular place for Oscar trophies."

"What?" Vincent asked.

"Oscar trophies. I hear a lot of actors and actresses keep them in the bathroom." My phone buzzed in my hand, but I didn't recognize the number. I ignored it. If it was important, they'd leave a message. I turned the corner and noticed the plumbers sitting on the deck in front of Caralt's house. I raised my hand and they waved back.

"Hey guys, what's up?" I asked as I got closer.

They didn't look like they were on a break. They looked too annoyed for that.

"Some police detective is in there with Caralt," the foreman said. "Said we should wait out here."

My eyes went wide. "That's so weird."

A detective? What were the chances it was...

I craned my neck to see over the shoulder of the

biggest guy. Yep. I could barely make Detective Lee out through the large windows facing the canal.

"He probably got some shit stolen," another guy said. "With all the renovations to this place, he's had people tromping in and out of this house for weeks."

"Huh."

"And he's got a lot of stuff that'd be easy to sell," the third man said quietly.

The rest of us looked at him.

"Just saying," he said with a shrug. "All that collectible stuff, right? I mean, he's even got it in the bathrooms. We had to move a bunch of it out so it wouldn't get wrecked. He's way careful with that shit."

I nodded, but in the back of my head I was wondering if the delay would keep the plumbers there for another few days. I wouldn't mind that, even if they did listen to Nickelback.

A few minutes later, Detective Lee must have left because Caralt came to the french doors and pulled them open.

"Gentlemen, my apologies." His eyes landed on me. "Gentlemen and *Linx*. Linx, I tried to call you and let you know there had been a delay, but you didn't answer your phone."

"Sorry. I didn't mind waiting. No biggie."

He nodded, then creepy Leo Caralt disappeared inside.

The foreman said, "No explanation, huh?"

The second man said, "This dude is weird."

"You can say that again," I muttered under my

breath. Didn't matter. It was time to work, and I needed to get to it.

I walked up to the library and immediately reached for the brushes and paints I'd cleaned and left on the worktable the day before. Everything was where I'd left it. I'd wondered if Creepy Leo would look through my things after he found me in the bathroom. If he did, it wasn't apparent.

"Okay," I whispered. "Work time."

It was Frank's—and now Vincent's—cue to leave me alone. As soon as I picked up my brush, I forgot about Caralt. I forgot about Vincent and Gabby dying. I forgot about all that and let myself fall into the mural.

I loved this piece, and it didn't matter how I felt about the person commissioning it. That was the thing about commissions. Some artists got snooty about painting within parameters, but not me. I considered it a challenge.

Several hours later, I was working on the woman in the mural. I still hadn't decided if she was beckoning with a finger or threatening with a gun.

"Come hither or stay away?" I muttered under my breath.

"Come hither."

I turned to the voice in the corner. It was Caralt. I hadn't heard him come in, but he was leaning against the wall, arms crossed, staring at the painting I was working on.

No, that's not creepy. Not at all.

Was it? Or was I overreacting? It *was* his house. I

tried to kill the goose bumps on my neck so I could be pleasant with a client.

"Hey," I said. "So you're voting come hither?"

He smiled, and it actually reached his eyes. "It's your choice. You've brought this room to life with this piece. I don't want to interfere at this point. It was just a thought."

I shrugged. "It's your room."

His eyes roamed around the space. "It's your painting."

"I haven't decided yet," I said. "I'm open to ideas. Why come hither?"

"What man hasn't imagined a beautiful woman desiring him?" he asked. "Men like me aren't usually the kind to attract female attention. Not on our own. It's only after we're older... when we're successful. Have money. Have something they want. That's when they show an interest."

They, huh? Was he talking about Gabby? Even if he wasn't, I wanted to curl my lip. Caralt struck me as the kind of man who thought women owed him something. My gut told me he saw women as prizes or trophies— flawless figures in see-through boxes—not real, living people.

I turned back to the wall. "Yeah, I don't know about that. I wasn't ever considered the beautiful girl myself."

"You're kidding." His voice was warm and jovial, as if he hadn't just insulted half the population. "You're gorgeous."

Oh, I'm so flattered.

I didn't say that. Even though I found him skin-crawly, he was still a client. "Thank you."

"You probably had the boys *begging* after you in high school."

Gross. I set down my brush and turned around. "No, actually. I was the weird girl in school and dropped out of middle school because of bullying. I only survived high school because my best friend scared the popular kids away. But that's fine. I grew up and realized that everyone is a punk when they're young and still developing their frontal lobe." I smiled and turned back to work. Where was my bogie? I always felt more confident if he was around. Even if he couldn't do anything, he made me brave.

"I guess you're a bigger person than me." Caralt's voice was distinctly less warm.

"Just learned a few hard lessons over the years. No use dwelling on the past."

I didn't hear him walk in the room, but I heard him walking out.

The girl in the painting was definitely getting a gun.

———

I WAS SITTING in my backyard, drinking a beer and staring at Bogie. "He did it."

Vincent said, "I thought we knew that already."

"I still harbored a few doubts, but I don't anymore."

Frank cocked his head. "What changed?"

"I couldn't wrap my head around a guy like Caralt murdering for comic books. Even as big a collector as he is, he has to have insurance, right? He's a businessman too. Very successful. Why would he risk everything to get his comics back?"

Frank said, "He's obsessive and smart? Thinks he's above the law?"

I shook my head. "I don't think it was about the baseball cards. Or the theft. Not really." I sipped my beer. "I think he found out Gabby was after him for his collection. She didn't like him, she liked his comic collection—or the money she could get from it anyway. And she's not after his money the traditional way either. She steals from him. That's what really set him off. The insult to his ego, not the theft."

"Either way, he killed 'em," Frank said.

I nodded. "Yep."

"We have anything concrete enough to take to Detective Lee?"

"Nope."

Vincent said, "I wish I could remember what happened."

"We know what happened," I said. "Roughly. You guys stole from him, he found out—"

"But how did he find out?" Frank said.

"Hmm?"

"How did Caralt figure out who was behind the theft?"

"It's just a guess," I said, "but a really cute girl started to cuddle up to him, he tells her about his super-awesome-amazing comic book collection, then the collection gets stolen. I'm guessing he put two and two together."

Vincent said, "Then he goes and hunts us down?" The ghost rubbed his hands over his arms. "That's so cold."

"How did he find Gabby?" Frank asked. "Would Gabby have taken a mark to her own place?"

"No way," Vincent said. "Maybe the comic book shop? They might have her address. But they might have her parents' because she was living there when she started working at the shop."

I said, "I don't think Caralt would want anyone knowing he was asking around about Gabby. He's not dumb. He wants his comics back and he wants revenge on the girl who insulted him. He might not have even planned to kill her. I don't know."

"Records searches can be done on the computer now," Frank said. "You and I do them all the time. He's a computer guy, right?"

I nodded. "As long as there was something in her own name attached to her current address, he might have been able to find her."

"Gabby didn't own much," Vincent said. "She lived with a roommate, and the apartment was in her room-mate's name because she was there first. Gabby just wrote her a check for her share of the rent. I remember them arguing about it on the phone and her roommate getting pissed because if Gabby was late with rent, it was affecting the roommate's credit score or something like that."

"Okay, so her name wasn't listed on her apartment," Frank said. "She own a car?"

"Yeah," Vincent said. "But her license and stuff was

still registered at her parents' house because I remember her complaining about her registration renewal going there and it was late because her mom didn't call her. And it's not like her mom would have told anyone where Gabby was because she and Gabby were not—"

"Vincent." I broke in. "Focus."

I finished my beer and thought about grabbing another. "Sounds like Gabby was pretty savvy about staying under the radar."

My thoughts went again to the very well-organized storage unit. This girl was not a newcomer to theft. She had a bookkeeping system in that desk. She had inventory. She had…

"The storage unit." Frank and I spoke at the same time.

"Oh, she had the storage unit before we met," Vincent said.

I stared at Frank. "It was hers. She wouldn't want her parents knowing. No roommate was going to rent it for her."

Frank said, "The storage unit would have been in her name. I bet you a pack of Lucky Strikes that's what Caralt found."

I ignored the bet because there was no reason for me to smoke on this case. Frank would have to live without his precious cigarettes for a while. "Vincent, did you and Gabby ever work late at the unit doing inventory or selling stuff? Anything like that? Would she have been there alone?"

"She might have been. I went with her sometimes.

Sorting all the comics took time. I helped, but I know sometimes she'd go by herself."

Frank said, "We were looking at the storage unit as a secondary crime scene. It might be the primary."

Vincent asked, "What does that mean?"

"It means that if the storage unit was the only thing Gabby had in her name, then that's probably what Leo Caralt found. And if he found the address and the unit, he might have found her. That storage unit wasn't just where you two kept your take," I said. "It might also be where you were killed."

7

Using Loved Ones for Dastardly Plans

I WAS BACK at Caralt's the next day, more determined than ever to finish the mural while the plumbers were still there. I did not want to be alone with Creepy Leo. I could feel Frank and Vincent hanging out, but I couldn't see them. Every now and then, I'd get a whisper from the two ghosts, but they mostly left me to my thoughts.

When I was painting, my mind entered this really clear place, especially when I was doing lines. I was focused on the details, but at the same time, my brain could wander, especially on murals where there was so much busywork. That morning, I let my mind roam to what I knew and what steps I could take that would make Leo Caralt land in a jail cell.

I suspected Caralt had killed Gabby in the storage unit. I also suspected that's where Vincent had found them, either in the act or right after. How had Gabby been killed? That I didn't know.

You need to call Raul.

I knew there was evidence tying Vincent to a crime at Caralt's—the baseball cards in the safe—but I didn't know if that was enough to make him a suspect in their deaths.

The police had already found the storage unit, but had they linked it to the murder? Was there any forensic evidence there?

You could plant some.

Yes, but what to plant?

I really needed to talk to Raul. Would his sense of justice be enough to overcome his anger with me? Calling him was a bad idea. Texting him was a worse idea. I needed to ambush him if I wanted him to listen. I grabbed my phone and called Nan.

"Lindsay? Is everything all right?"

I put my brush down. "Yeah. Why do you sound like that?"

"You never call, love. I assumed something must be wrong."

She was right. I usually texted. "No, I'm fine, but Raul is pissed at me."

"I know dear. I wish there was something—"

"Can you call Grann Paulette and tell her to invite Raul to dinner at her house? Maybe… make it a requirement for her continued love and good graces?"

"Does she know why he's angry with you?"

"I have no idea. But I can ambush him there and make him talk to me if I know when he'll be at her house." Grann Paulette lived just a few blocks from my nan and me.

"I'm on it," Nan said. "We'll sort this out, love. Just

finish that mural for that awful man as quickly as you can. I hate that you're working at that house."

"Trust me, I feel exactly the same way."

I hung up and picked up my brush and paintpot again. I'd finished the gun, and that had been the last design element. With the major blocks of color finished and most of the shading done, the rest was all line work, and because it was manga inspired, the line work was all black. I didn't need to worry about texture; this style needed to be as flat as possible. So after the line work and a little more shading, I'd be finished. I could kiss the creepy action figure dungeon goodbye and leave Leo Caralt to his eventual arrest. If I could stay focused, I'd finish in about two more days.

Which didn't leave me much time for snooping.

I needed to find out how Gabby was killed. Vincent had been an overdose, but had he used the same method on Gabby? If Leo had surprised Gabby at the storage unit, how had he found Vincent? Vincent would have fought back. He was pretty built and would have been more than a match for Leo Caralt. That meant Leo had surprised Vincent in some way and overpowered him.

My thoughts were too chaotic. I needed to simplify.

Talk to Raul. Find out Gabby's cause of death.

Convince Detective Lee to go back to the storage unit and go over it with a fine-tooth comb.

…something, something, something…

Creepy Leo lands in jail.

I had this. Totally, totally had this. I just needed to find out what the "something" was.

The   plumbing   foreman   walked   into   the

office. "Hey!"

I turned and smiled. "Hey yourself. What's up?"

There hadn't been too much socializing between me and the guys working on the bathrooms. Other than the occasional inquiry about which facilities were open for business, we kept out of each other's way.

The foreman looked around. "That painting is really cool. The rest…"

I could see him noticing all the boxed action figures in their tiny clear prisons.

I whispered, "It's a little weird."

He looked relieved. My thoughts must have mirrored his own. "I can't imagine working in here."

"Yeah, I'll be happy to be done."

He narrowed his eyes and dropped his voice. "Yeah, about that…"

"You guys are nearly finished yourself, right?"

He stepped closer and crossed burly, tattooed arms covered in silver hair. "I got a daughter about your age."

I frowned. "Okay. Cool."

"And I'm thinkin' maybe only a couple of us are gonna be able to be here tomorrow, you know? With those cops visiting… How much longer you think you'll be working on this painting?"

"Two, maybe three days. But I'm hoping for two."

He nodded. "I'm gonna leave my card for you. And you call me when you're gonna be here, you get me? It'll probably be more… convenient for everyone if there was someone in the house with you when you're work-ing. Make sure you're not using any bathrooms that aren't finished and all."

My eyes went wide. Did the plumber just offer to babysit me while I was working at Leo's?

"So what you're saying is that if I'm going to be here for another three days, you think that's about when you guys are finishing up too?"

He shrugged. "That sounds about right."

I had a feeling from looking at their work they could be done by the end of the day if they wanted.

"I don't want to cause any trouble," I said quietly.

The foreman grinned. "You know plumbers. We work on our own schedule, you know? Sometimes we get emergencies. Can't help that."

Bless him. Bless him. Bless him. All Nickelback love was forgiven if I didn't have to worry about being in Caralt's home by myself.

"Three days," I said. "I think that lines up with my schedule."

"You just make sure it does." He pulled a bent business card from his back pocket. "I'll leave this here by your backpack, all right?"

"Thanks…"

"I'm Manny. My son is the younger version of me with the beard. His name is Junior. You just let us know and we'll take care of stuff, you get me?"

"I get you," I said. "And my name is Linx. Thanks."

"No problem, Linx. Cool name."

"Thanks," I whispered. "Really thanks."

He looked around the room. "That painting is very good. You got a gift, young lady."

Sometimes—not always, but sometimes—people were awesome.

———

GRANN PAULETTE SHOVED Raul out the door and onto the porch. "Go talk to your friend."

"Grann—"

"You want my *accras*, you go fix things with your girl." She shut the door behind him.

I sat on the porch, rocking back and forth on the swing that faced the walking street in front of Grann Paulette's house. She had lived on the narrow walking street past Electric Avenue for as long as I'd been alive, and her garden was an eclectic combination of vegetables, sculpture, and flowers that had always filled me with envy.

Raul had grown up with his grandmother the same way I'd grown up with mine.

"Hi," I said.

"You could have texted me."

"You wouldn't have answered."

"You could have called."

I turned toward him. "And you could have called, but you didn't. And you weren't going to."

He sat next to me and pursed his lips. "I would have."

"How long?"

"Eventually."

I shook my head. "Eventually doesn't work for me. Are you mad because I lied to you or because you think I'm nuts?"

He took a deep breath. "Linx… I am a scientist."

"And I'm an artist. You think I don't feel kind of nuts about all this too?"

He didn't say anything.

"Okay, tell me this. All these years, when my nan or my mom mentioned seeing spirits or hearing them, did you just think they were lying? Or crazy?"

He motioned back in the house. "I thought they were eccentric. Like her. The woman who goes to mass five times a week and lights a candle to Saint Anthony for my dad, who's never coming back, Linx. Sometimes you accept people are who they are and… that's all. But you're asking me to believe you—my best friend since we were fifteen—can see souls and spirits. For real?"

"Yes, for real." I felt tears prick my eyes. "So you think my nan is a liar. Think my mom is nuts. Think that I'm crazy too."

"No, I don't think you are, and that's why I'm freaked out!" He dropped his voice. "I mean, aren't you?"

"No," I said. "I'm Ghost Girl, remember? I've been living with this since I was thirteen. And I don't see them every now and then like my nan and my mom. I see one spirit. All the time. His name is Frank Bogle, and he was a detective in the LAPD. He was killed in the line of duty in 1953. And he bugs the shit out of me to help him solve random crimes every now and then."

I felt Frank appear over my shoulder. "Keep going, kid. You're doing great. Raul will come around."

Raul said, "So that's why you're always asking me weird questions, huh? Because you're some kind of ghost detective?"

I covered my face with my hands. "Not... I don't solve mysteries for ghosts. I just, you know, every now and then Frank sees something or something falls in our lap. And we solve it. You know, just looking into things."

"Like this Vincent and Gabby thing?"

"Vincent is a first," I whispered. "I *am* freaked out about that. Because from the time I was a kid, it was just Frank and me. That's the only ghost I've ever seen. And he's pretty normal."

"*Pretty* normal?" Frank asked. "Kid, I'm not the one with pink hair."

"And then Mrs. L tells me there's a body in the boat behind her house," I continued, "and suddenly Vincent is there telling me he didn't do any drugs. He's dead, but he's there."

"And that's the part that freaked you out?" Raul's eyes went wide. "Not being followed around by a ghost since the time you were— I cannot believe I am even saying this." His head dropped back on the porch swing. "Linx, this is nuts."

"You know I'm not lying."

"I don't know that, because if you're telling me the truth right now, that means you've been lying for over ten years, Linds."

He never called me Linds unless he was really upset. When he broke up with his first real boyfriend, he called me Linds. When he got a letter from his dad, he called me Linds.

Raul was really upset.

"So who am I supposed to believe, huh? Lindsay then or Lindsay now?"

"I don't know what to tell you," I said. "I wanted…" I sighed. I was sick to my stomach. I understood why he was angry, but I didn't know how to explain a fifteen-year-old's reasoning.

Raul said, "What did you want? Explain it to me."

"When we were kids, I wanted a normal thing. A normal place and person. You and Grann Paulette were the place. You were the person."

He looked over his shoulder. The smell of fried plantains drifted out the window, and Grann Paulette was singing along at the top of her lungs to Cesária Évora. Only it was in Portuguese, not French, so half of the words she mumbled. Though music streamed through the house, the radio was tuned to the Spanish news station.

"This place was your normal?" he asked. "I suddenly feel more sorry for you than pissed."

I shrugged. "You didn't talk about weird ghosts you'd had to deal with or why the dry cleaner on Venice and Main was off-limits."

Raul furrowed his eyebrows. "I use that cleaner."

"Which is fine, but if you're my gran, you have to listen to the foulmouthed ghost who lives in the building and likes to make lewd comments about women's dresses."

Raul had nothing to say to that.

"All I'm saying is that I wanted a normal friend. You were my normal friend. You didn't look at me and see Ghost Girl. You saw me and liked me. And when we first met, you were the only one who did. Do you really think I was going to mess that up by telling you I had the ghost of a dead cop hanging around me all the time?"

"That would have put a damper on all the trespassing when we were kids."

"Trust me, I got an earful after every fence jump. Frank hates it when I do illegal shit."

Raul sat and rocked his heels back and forth, swinging us as the radio blared and more and more delicious smells drifted from Grann Paulette's kitchen.

He said, "I understand why you wouldn't tell me."

"But you're never going to see me the same way," I said quietly.

"Linx, how can I?" He turned to me. His eyes were soft and pled for my understanding. "How can I?"

"I'm the same person I was before you knew."

"But if I accept what you're saying and believe you... then *I'm* not the same person."

I nodded and stood, my heart fallen to my stomach. I shouldn't have rushed this. I should have given him more time.

"What do you need?" he asked quietly. "You wouldn't have done this—asked my grandmother for a favor to see me—unless you needed something."

"You're right."

He grimaced. "So what do you need?"

"Gabby's cause of death. I know she was dumped in the marina, but—"

"Drowning," he said. "But we got the toxicology back. She had a lethal dose of heroin in her system. She would have died just like Vincent if she hadn't been thrown in the water. We found needle marks in her vein.

Bruises on her arm. She was held down and injected. She didn't have any other marks, so it's likely that she'd never used heroin before. It probably would have taken effect in seconds."

"And Vincent?"

"Again within seconds. But injecting someone who's fighting you off is probably pretty difficult."

"So he'd have used something to knock them out?"

"Probably?"

"Could you use chloroform?" I asked.

Raul laughed. "Do you really think I know what it would take to knock someone out, Linx? Ask your ghost detective guy."

Frank muttered, "Ether's more likely than chloroform. And probably easier to get. Especially if all you want to do is knock someone out and you don't care about making them sick."

"Would ether show up on a toxicology report?" I asked.

Raul shook his head. "Not unless we were testing for it."

"Got it." I mulled over the new information. So Leo had injected both Gabby and Vincent with enough heroin to kill them. "Is Leo an addict? How did he get his hands on that much heroin?"

"Who's Leo?"

"The tech executive that I'm doing the mural for."

"Wait, that's who you think killed these two people?" Raul's eyes were the size of saucers. "And you're working for him? *What are you doing?*"

"I'm investigating Vincent's death so that hopefully

he'll leave me alone! You think I want another ghost hanging around me all the time? No offense, Frank."

"None taken," Bogie muttered. "That kid can get annoying."

Raul said, "So you're investigating the guy you're working for? Are you sure that's a good idea? I mean, if you're right, then you're working for a murderer."

I muttered, "I didn't know he was a murderer when I accepted the job."

"I think you need to tell Detective Lee about this," Raul said.

"Sure." I snorted. "Hey, superhot cop. I know who killed Gabby and Vincent. I don't have any proof or anything, but I'm pretty sure I know."

"Isn't there anything that might set him on the right track?" Raul said. "I do not like you working for this guy."

"Don't worry. The plumbers have me covered," I said under my breath, all the while thinking about what Raul had said.

"I don't even know what that means," Raul said. "Why are you talking about plumbers? Call the police."

Isn't there anything that might set him on the right track?

Was there? I'd already told Detective Lee I could see Vincent's ghost. I mean, he already thought I was crazy. Maybe I could just call him up and tell him I thought the murder had happened at the ministorage. He'd probably ignore me, but maybe he wouldn't.

Either way, it was worth a shot.

———

"DETECTIVE CHRISTOPHER LEE," a voice answered.

I was expecting to hear the follow-up in his deep, sexy voice. *I'm not at my desk right now. Please leave me a message.*

Nope. No message. It was really the dreamy detective.

"Why are you working so late?" I sputtered. "I was just going to leave a voice mail."

He paused. "Linx?"

"I didn't think you'd be working at"—I glanced at the clock—"two in the morning. Why are you working at two a.m.?"

"Why are you calling at two a.m.?" he asked. "Is everything all right?"

"I… Yes, I'm all right. I had an idea."

Long silence.

"You had an idea at two in the morning and decided to call me?" he finally asked. "What… what kind of idea?"

Was his voice deeper? What kind of idea was he hoping for?

"Um… I actually had the idea earlier in the day, but I didn't want to bother you, so I was calling when I thought you'd be gone."

"So you're avoiding me."

I said, "Didn't you tell me I shouldn't be interesting?"

"Yeah, that was impossible advice," he muttered.

I sat up straight on my bed. "Wait, what?"

"I just mean you're…" He sighed. "What was your idea, Linx?"

Okay, we're leaving the passive-aggressive flirtation alone. Probably a good idea.

I tried to sound official. "I have reason to believe that Gabby and Vincent were both killed at the ministorage."

"You mean the one where you *don't* have a storage unit?"

"I have no idea what you're talking about. I have just been informed—"

"By a ghost?"

"I told you he was hanging around. Why you gotta make it weird, Detective?"

Did I hear muffled laughter on the other end of the phone?

Detective Lee said, "So Vincent's ghost told you that's where he was killed?"

Okay, he definitely sounded amused. Amused was better than dismissive.

"No, he told me the storage unit was the only thing Gabby had in her name. Her apartment was in her roommate's name. Her car was registered at her parents' address. The only thing that was only registered to Gabby was that storage unit. So if someone went looking for her because someone thought they'd been robbed, then that's what they'd find. And it was pretty evident that someone had been in the unit. Vincent seemed to think a lot was missing and had been moved around. Like maybe after a struggle?"

Another long silence.

"That's a very perceptive line of reasoning," Detective Lee said.

"I'm not an idiot or a crazy person," I said. "I promise."

He let out a long breath. "You remember I asked Chuck Morrissey about you?"

"Yeah."

"I guess… It sounds like sometimes your grand-mother would call him."

My eyes went wide. "She what?"

"She'd sometimes *know* things about cases. Recent cases. Old cases. Didn't want to be officially involved, she said. She just had hunches. Probably from knowing the city so well. Intuition kind of stuff. From living in the city and knowing people, you know?"

How had I never heard this before? I mean, I wasn't surprised, but I was kind of surprised.

"Chuck said your grandmother never wanted her name mentioned. But that sometimes… she was helpful. That was all he said."

"Are you saying that it's possible I just have a hunch? That something happened in the ministorage?"

"You grew up here," he said carefully. "You're clearly very perceptive."

"You're… probably right. It's a hunch." *And you defi-nitely do not have a pet psychic, Detective Lee.*

"I'll send a team back to the storage unit," he said. "Just to make sure we didn't miss anything."

"Cool. That's great."

"So why were you really calling at two a.m.? Were you out adding to your somewhat impressive trespassing record?"

"You looked up my record?" I asked. "I didn't know

you cared, Detective. And I'd call it more than '*somewhat impressive.*'"

"Linx."

"Fine. I just got back from my friend Raul's house. His grandmother is Haitian and she cooks amazing food. Dinners there are not short events."

"I don't think I've ever had amazing food. Sorry, Haitian food." He yawned. "I've had amazing food before."

I smiled. "You sound tired. Why are you still working?"

"Paperwork. Every cop's favorite pastime. Is Raul your boyfriend?"

My eyebrows went up. "It would be news to his current boyfriend if he were. No, we've been friends since high school though. He's family."

"That's nice."

"So…" I took a chance. "No family waiting up for you, huh? No wife or girlfriend?"

He laughed a little. "No. Was I that obvious when I asked?"

"Just obvious enough to make me curious."

His voice was definitely lower. "You were already curious."

I nearly bounced up and down on my bed. "And I was already interesting."

He let out something that sounded like a throaty growl. I silently screamed, *Oh my god, so sexy!* in my head.

"Linx, this is… not a good idea."

"Because you think I'm crazy?"

"Because you're involved in an open investigation."

"So you don't think I'm crazy?"

"I never…" He yawned. "I don't think you're crazy. You see a lot on this job you can't explain. I may not be a rule-breaker, but I try to keep an open mind."

"What should I call you at two in the morning?" I mused. "I mean, if I call during office hours, I'll call you Detective Lee."

"Are you going to call during office hours?"

I stretched out on my bed. "I don't know. You're a little easier to talk to in the middle of the night."

"Are you in bed right now?"

"You have good ears." I closed my eyes. "Christopher Lee. Christopher is a mouthful. Chris? Chris suits you. Please don't say Topher, because then I'll have to judge you horribly."

His chuckle was low and rough. "Just Chris."

"Chris."

"Yeah." His voice got all growly again. "Just Chris. I'm going to send you my mobile number. If you need to tell me another…"

"Hunch?" My phone buzzed against my head. I glanced down and saw an unknown number with the simple message *It's me.* He'd just texted me his mobile number while I was on the phone with him. I officially had Detective Sexy's digits.

"Call me on this number," he said. "Or you can text me."

"Do I need to text you?"

He paused. "You tell me."

8

The Part Where I Piss Everyone Off

"IT'S COMING ALONG NICELY."

I looked over my shoulder. Creepy Leo was standing in the doorway.

"Thanks."

Bogie had been leaning against the far wall, whistling a Nina Simone tune under his breath. He stopped whistling and stood straight.

"It's nice to know someone keeps to a professional schedule." Leo turned his head toward the bathroom where I could hear Junior and another guy chatting loudly over the blaring radio. "I'm sorry they're still bothering you."

I shrugged and went back to work. "They're fine." I wanted to finish this mural, not chat with a guy who'd murdered two people.

I know. Such a diva.

"It looks finished."

"It's not," I said. "Not quite." I got that a lot toward

the end of a mural like this, because the fill was done. Most of it was finished, but it was the details that often tripped you up. A few outlines. Some shadows. Simple stuff that always took longer than you thought it would.

I heard him walk into the room. "When will you be finished?"

"I'm hoping before the weekend."

"Well, if you want to work tonight, I have an event to attend, so you're more than welcome to stay late. You wouldn't be bothering me."

I nodded but didn't give him a response. I felt Bogie move toward me. I knew he couldn't really do anything, but I still felt better knowing he was close.

"You have your personal security code." Leo's voice sounded pinched. He was probably annoyed I wasn't giving him my undivided attention. "So I'll leave the system in guest mode while I'm gone. I'll be alerted when you come and go, of course."

"Okay, cool."

That was one of the convenient (weird?) things about working for Caralt. I didn't have a key to the place, but I did have my own security code that would let me into the house. That meant I could get in anytime if Leo allowed the system to let workmen or guests in. That also meant he could track my movements when I came and went.

"So will you be working tonight?" he asked.

Bogie said, "Don't even think about it, kid."

I stopped and took the opportunity to stretch my back before I turned around. Leo Caralt definitely looked annoyed, but I'd pacified him by turning and giving him my absolute attention. "I might try to come in, but it'll depend on if my grandmother needs my help tonight."

There. I'd left open the possibility, but also given myself an out. I was leaning toward Bogie's suggestion anyway.

"Ah." Leo nodded stiffly. "What would your grandmother need help with?"

I frowned. Leo had never asked me personal questions.

Bogie didn't have to be as polite as I did. "I don't know, asshole," he said. "Dinner, maybe? Finger painting? Macramé? How about none of your damn business?"

Leo seemed to understand he'd overstepped when I didn't answer. "As I said, I'll leave the house in guest mode so you'll be able to enter should you want to. I'll be home at midnight, so if you decide to work, please be finished by then."

"Oh, can she be?" Frank asked. "Can she, you pitiful creep? I'm so sick of this guy's shit. I say we call Detective Lee now and tell him about Vincent's safe."

I had to find a way to make sure those baseball card frames were still up there before I let Detective Lee know where they were in Vincent's house. I had no idea if Leo had reported them as stolen. Finding them would mean nothing unless I could tie them to Caralt.

I ignored Bogie and smiled at Leo. "I'll make sure to text you if I end up coming over." I turned back to the wall and hoped the conversation was over.

It wasn't.

"Do you often help your grandmother?"

My eyes went wide. Good God, was Creepy Leo trying to make small talk?

"She's older," I said. "I do what I can." *Please go away.*

"That's very thoughtful."

I started on another long line and prayed he'd get the hint.

He didn't.

"Living in proximity to younger family members must be an advantage for the elderly as they decline."

Something in the clinical way he made the statement made me stop and turn around. Caralt was standing by the door, his hands in his pockets, a nearly human expression in his normally cold eyes.

"Of course," he continued, "if you've treated your children or grandchildren badly, they are less likely to be invested in your ongoing health."

Something told me Leo Caralt's family hadn't exactly been the Waltons.

Bogie seemed to agree. "This guy has issues," he said. "Still doesn't give him an excuse to murder. Plenty of people have shit families and don't turn into murderers."

"My family is great." I tried to smile. "I'm really lucky to have a grandmother close enough to visit." Something in me didn't want Caralt knowing too much about my family or where I lived.

Something in his eyes told me he already did.

An expression of smug amusement flashed across his face. "Have a nice *visit* with your grandmother."

"Have fun at your party." I turned back to the wall as Leo walked down the stairs to the first floor.

"Creep," Bogie said.

I needed to finish this painting, but I sure as hell did not want to be in Caralt's house alone.

Then again...

I couldn't help glancing at the stairwell that led to the third floor. The one with the weird bathroom. The one with all the baseball stuff. The one Leo Caralt definitely didn't want me exploring.

Shit.

———

"OF ALL THE harebrained ideas you've had over the years, kid, this is one of the worst." Bogie was pacing back and forth in my room.

"I basically have permission to be at his house when he's gone," I said. "He practically invited me over."

"But doesn't that seem like a bad idea?" Vincent asked, his eyes the size of saucers. "I'm not a detective, but I agree with Frank here. This seems really dangerous."

"Well, so is breaking into people's houses, Vincent, but that didn't stop you, did it?"

Frank glared at me. "And you notice what happened to him?"

My room was not the most spacious. Therefore, having two ghosts—one of whom was pacing—keeping me company as I painted my toenails and contemplated burglary was not giving me the Zen focus I was aiming for with the pedicure.

"We need evidence that Caralt wanted to kill Vincent. The best evidence we have is those cards you stole and locked in your safe. But unless he reported them stolen—"

"Do we know he didn't?" Frank asked.

I paused. I actually didn't know. I'd never found out why Detective Lee was at his house the other day. Maybe he'd been reporting the baseball stuff stolen? If that was the case, linking Leo and Vincent would be easy. I picked up my phone and texted Detective Sexy.

What? What nickname was I supposed to give him in my phone?

I texted: *Why were you at Leo Caralt's house the other day?*

He texted back far quicker than I'd expected: *Are you still working there?*

Yes.

The phone rang almost immediately. Detective Sexy flashed on the screen along with a very grainy picture I'd ninja-ed at Vincent's crime scene.

Don't judge me; I wanted to show Raul.

"Why are you still working there?" Detective Lee asked.

"Uh, because I'm a professional who agreed to do a job for the man, and honestly"—I finished my pinky toe and put the cap back on the bottle of nail polish—"if I stopped now, it would just bug the shit out of me until I finished because I cannot stand not finishing my work."

"Is that why you got arrested three times at the same building when you were twenty?"

"One, I cannot believe you actually looked that up, and two, I have pictures of that piece. If I showed it to you, you'd understand."

"And you couldn't put it on a canvas?"

"Do you have a twenty-foot canvas lying around I could borrow? Thanks! That would be great."

He sighed loudly. "Cut the shit, Linx. Why are you still working for Caralt?"

"I'm almost done. Did he report things stolen?"

"I can't tell you that."

I spread my toes, admiring the bright purple, and ignored Bogie's expression, which told me he did not appreciate that I wasn't putting Detective Lee on speakerphone. "Let's just say I know that he might have had some comics and collectibles stolen."

Detective Lee was carefully silent.

"But let's say I also know about some other things that were stolen."

"Money?" he asked.

"No."

"Art?"

"Define art."

"Is this a philosophical debate? Because I don't really have time to—"

"Baseball cards." I leaned my head against the wall. "Did he mention anything about baseball cards?"

Bogie whispered, "A signed *Mickey Mantle* rookie card."

I waved him away and waited for Detective Lee's response.

"I don't know anything about missing baseball cards," he said. "That guy collects baseball cards?"

"I know, it surprised me too. He has one bathroom that's super weird and—"

"Don't go snooping around Caralt," he said firmly. "I'm not joking about this, Linx. Do not do it." His voice dropped to a near-whisper. "I don't even like you working for this guy."

"Are you still at the office?"

"Yeah."

"Okay." It was early. That made sense. I glanced at the window. It was early. The sun was still out. It was six o'clock. It was still light.

What was it about daylight made everything seem less dangerous?

"Okay, so… you're going to keep your mobile phone on you tonight, right? Or do you, like, go to the gym after work or something like that?" He probably went to the gym. He looked like the type.

Detective Sexy said, "I go in the morning. What are you going to do?"

Nailed it. "Nothing."

"Linx, you better not—"

"Have a great night, Chris! Sorry, office hours." I hopped up from the bed. "Have a great night, Detective Sexy. I will talk to you later."

"Linx—"

"Okay, bye." I hung up before he could say another word.

So this was the part where I pissed everyone off.

———

DID I know it was a bad idea?

Yeah, pretty much. But I knew it was a bad idea the same way I knew breaking and entering was a bad idea. I knew it… I was just foolishly optimistic.

Breaking into Leo Caralt's house that night was far easier than most building sites. After all, I had a code! I had a reason to be there. All I had to do was go to Leo's office.

Which I did.

Pick up my brushes and paints.

Which I did.

And stay away from the third-floor bathroom.

I did not do that.

I picked up my brushes and paints, set them down again. Glanced around the office lined with tiny plastic people in their tiny plastic prisons.

And realized I *really* hated Leo Caralt.

I hated that he'd killed two people, and I still had to put up with him hovering over my shoulder. I hated that I knew he'd done it and he was still walking around being smug. I knew police work took time. I knew correct procedures were important.

I also knew that wherever Leo was that night, it wasn't in that house.

Putting my brushes and paintpot down, I walked toward the stairs.

Bogie appeared in front of me. "Go home."

"I get a picture of that bathroom. I get a picture of the frame with the missing cards and I send it to Detective Lee with the combination to Vincent's safe, and the police have a tie between them."

"I didn't teach you better than this?" he hissed. "You don't get to take shortcuts, Linx. This stuff takes time. You need warrants. You can't just—"

"All I'm doing is going to the bathroom." I walked through him and felt the chill cover my body. All I was doing was going upstairs and taking a picture. All I had to do was confirm that the frame was still there and send a picture to Detective Lee.

The problem was, when I walked down the hall and opened the doorway, every bit of baseball memorabilia was gone.

"Shit."

Bogie appeared beside me. "Leave. Leave now."

"Okay, I kinda figured the frame with the missing rookie card would be gone, but the whole bathroom?"

"Kid, you need to leave."

"There was all this stuff." I turned around in the small space. "Where did it go?" I marched out of the bathroom and headed for the only other door on the third floor. I was pissed. I was sick of Leo Caralt, and I wanted someone to arrest him so I didn't have to see his smug face anymore. I turned the knob of the bedroom door, expecting it to be locked.

But it wasn't.

"Dammit, Linx!"

I walked inside and lights automatically turned on. I didn't think anything of it because the entire house was automated. Automatic lights. Automatic temperature control. Awful automatic toilet.

The room was immaculate and—just like its owner—weird. It was layers of black and white. Black floor, white rug. White sculptured headboard, black pillows. Pendants in chrome and black dropped from the ceiling, and a series of black-and-white nudes covered one wall. I was a firm believer in the beauty of the human form, but these were out there. Even for me.

In the center frame was a hairless model so pale she was nearly translucent, whose eyes and mouth were lined in white pigment. Next to it was another hairless model with dark umber skin whose eyes and mouth were lined in kohl. The same models repeated the series in different poses until the entire wall was filled. The women were like the action figures. Objects in clear cases, designed only to be observed.

There were no books, no pictures, nothing personal. Just a platform bed with drawers at the base, a dresser, and a wall of nude photographs.

Bogie turned in circles. "This one isn't right."

I had to agree, but I dropped to my knees and began opening drawers under the bed. Perfect lines of socks and underwear filled the one closest to the headboard.

"Linx, what are you doing?"

"He put that baseball stuff somewhere," I said. "We need to find it."

"We need to get the hell out of here. Wherever it is, it's not here."

Vincent appeared next to Bogie. "What are you doing?"

I opened the next drawer. White T-shirts lined up in more rows.

"You're not going to find anything here," Bogie nearly shouted. "Get out, Linx."

More drawers, more neat lines of clothing. I shut the last drawer and sat back on my heels.

Not the cards. We didn't need to find the baseball stuff. Hell, he might have already hidden the baseball stuff. Or sold it. Or...

Is Leo an addict? How did he get his hands on that much heroin?

I asked, "Where does an addict hide their stash?"

Vincent's eyes went wide. "You're asking me?"

I looked at Bogie. "Where?"

He looked even paler than his usual ghost self. "Where it's not gonna be found or where they need it the most."

Leo was smug and thought he was smarter than everyone. He'd probably think no one would see him as an addict. Would he be careless about his stash? This space was utterly organized. Utterly under his control.

So where was he out of control? Where did he need it the most?

I thought about the odd bathroom. About the crammed-in baseball memorabilia that fit nothing else in the house. Leo hadn't collected that stuff. Someone else had. Someone else, who'd collected it in the eighties when Leo was a kid.

... if you've treated your children or grandchildren badly...

I left the bedroom and walked back to the bathroom. Bogie followed me.

"Where?" I asked as I stood in the doorway.

"Try the toilet."

"The *toilet*?"

"The tank in back, Linx. Lift up the tank."

I lifted the back cover of the state-of-the-art self-flushing smart toilet and found a clean white box affixed to the back. It was hooked over the edge with two small white hooks and invisible unless the ceramic cover was removed.

"Pictures," Frank said. "Linx, take—"

"I got it." I pulled out my phone and snapped pictures of the toilet and the box before I lifted the edge. Inside, just as organized as the underwear drawer, were several small hypodermic needles in plastic wrapping and several small baggies of white powder along with a measuring spoon and a plain silver lighter. Also in the box were several prescription bottles. I left them in the bottom.

I took more pictures. It was opioid addiction in its most organized form. I tried to picture Leo Caralt shooting up, and I couldn't.

But there it was.

Maybe he only used the heroin and the needles when he was killing people. Maybe he used them on himself. Maybe—

I heard a door slam downstairs.

Maybe I was an idiot who had no patience.

I quickly replaced the toilet cover and walked out of the bathroom. I was good at running, but Leo's house didn't have any accessible windows on the third floor.

"Call the detective," Bogie said. "Call him now."

It was probably too much to hope that Leo was going to believe I was innocently using his bathroom again. Not after the last time he caught me. I could hear footsteps on the stairs, but they weren't in a hurry. I quickly texted the picture of the heroin to Detective Lee and shot him a short message as I walked down the stairs to Caralt's office.

Found this working at Caralt's. Help. Now.

I heard the soft tone that told me the picture delivered successfully as I slid the phone in my pocket and stepped into the office.

Leo Caralt was standing in the doorway with Bogie and Vincent flanking him.

"Hey," I said, as casually as I could. "Decided to get a little more done on the mural tonight."

"You didn't text me you'd be here," Caralt said, stepping into the room. He was wearing a long-sleeved black shirt buttoned to the neck and a pair of black slacks. A black tie completed the monotone look.

"Oh shoot." I stepped toward my brushes. "Sorry about that. I didn't think. I just used my code. Did you leave the party because the alarm went off or something?"

"Your code doesn't set off the house alarm," he said softly. "But the alarm on my bedroom door is another story."

9

A Lot of Questions Don't Have Answers

SHIT.

I'm sure my face went blank as my mind raced. Only the bullshitting skills that had saved me from dozens of trespassing charges saved me.

I felt my face heat up, but that was okay. Let Leo think I was embarrassed. "I'm sorry. I couldn't remember what room was the bathroom, and I—"

"You were in my bedroom for nearly five minutes." His face was stone-cold. "I certainly hope you didn't pee on my bed like a naughty dog."

What the hell was wrong with this man?

Bogie said, "Look for a way out. Forget the mural; you need a way out. You are not coming back here. Ever. Do you hear me?"

I was looking for a way out and an excuse, all at the same time. "Okay, you caught me." I tried for a laugh, but I was pretty sure it sounded fake. "My nan says I'm incorrigible. That means I don't know what's good for me, right? I'm too damn curious for my own good. I'm sorry, Leo."

He walked slowly toward me. "What were you looking for, Miss Maxwell?"

I slid to the side, inching toward the door. "Nothing really. Call me design curious, but the rest of your house is so cool, I was dying to know what your bedroom looked like. Those photographs, by the way—"

"I don't believe you." Leo's hand was in his pocket. It looked like it was clenched in a fist. "I don't believe a word coming out of your mouth. You knew them, didn't you?"

My eyes went wide. "What? Who?"

He frowned and shook his head. "I didn't... Why don't you really tell me why you took this job, Miss Maxwell?"

"I told you that you could call me Linx."

"I don't want to call you Linx!" He lunged toward me but pulled back before we collided. "We are not friends."

I couldn't hide my fear anymore. I felt myself shivering. "I'm going to leave. I'm sorry I came here tonight." I tried to move around him, but he reached out and grabbed my arm, digging his fingers into my elbow.

"You're not going anywhere."

"Let me go!" I tried to twist away, but he was a lot stronger than he looked.

"Give me your phone."

"Fuck you!" All pretense of politeness fled. "You're hurting me. Let go."

"Who are you working for? The police?"

"Are you insane?" I shouted. "Let me go or I'll call the police!"

Thank God I'd already called the police. I just hoped Detective Lee was already on the way. I could feel my phone buzzing in my pocket over and over again, but I ignored it. Leo was gripping my arm and it hurt.

Bogie slid next to me. I could feel his cool presence at my back. "Deep breaths," he said. "Don't panic. Twist to the right and pull down, kid."

I could hear the fear in Frank's voice, but his steady presence calmed me down. Leo wasn't very big, but he was strong. He was standing between me and the door. I twisted to the right, but he anticipated me. Leo pulled me into a bear hug and kicked the back of my knee, making my leg buckle.

"Why are you trying to get away?" he shouted. "What are you hiding?"

"I'm not hiding anything!" He'd grabbed my hair, forcing my head up at a painful angle.

"Fucking liar. All you bitches are liars," he screamed. "Every single one of you. She was a liar and then she stole from me. From *me*!"

"I don't know who you're talking about, you lunatic."

"I showed her though." He twisted me to the ground. "Just like I'll show you."

"You let me go now or I will scream this house down! Every neighbor on the canals—"

"Soundproofing, bitch." He spit in my ear. "Did you think you'd get away with what your friends couldn't?

They tried to steal from me, and I killed them. Just like I'm going to kill you."

We wrestled on the ground, Bogie and Vincent shouting around me. I tried to knee Leo in the groin, but he forced me to my side. I was squirming, but he was on top of me. Our fight wasn't cool or choreographed. I was shoving him off as well as I could. I knocked his head back with my elbow, but I got a fist in the eye. His knee was in my stomach.

"Linx, he's got a needle!" Vincent shouted. "Scream some more!"

"You bastard!" I yelled in his face. "You fucking insane bastard, let me go!" I turned my head and sank my teeth into his arm.

"Fuck you!"

"Linx, bite him again!"

I turned to the other side and bit harder, right on his shoulder. He screamed with pain or anger. Maybe both. I could feel the energy building in the room. There was something explosive happening. My body felt electrified.

Something hit the back of my head and fell to the floor.

Leo stopped and his eyes went wide. "What the fuck?"

I twisted away again and worked myself out from under his knee just in time to see one of Leo's action figure boxes fly through the air and whack him on the side of the head. His mouth dropped as more boxes flew at him. I rolled away and covered my head as the office filled with a whirlwind of boxes. They pelted Leo from every side, some of the plastic cutting his face. He curled into a ball on the ground as I crept toward the door. Just as the last of the boxes fell from the shelves, I heard a window break downstairs.

"Linx!"

Leo was shrieking in rage—"You told them! You told them!"—still covering his head as I heard heavy footsteps running up the stairs.

"LAPD! Get down, get down, get down!"

I couldn't hear anything after that.

———

THE BACK of an ambulance is not a comfortable place. I'd seen lots of cop shows that had witnesses hanging out there, wrapped in blankets while someone brought them some coffee and acted comforting.

That was not my experience.

"Do I get a blanket?" I asked Detective Lee. He was wearing a pair of jeans and a grey hoodie. It was the first time I'd seen him not wearing a suit.

"Do you need a blanket?" he asked. "It's like seventy-five degrees tonight."

"I guess not."

I sat and he hovered. Other people were going in and out of Leo Caralt's house, bringing in cameras and lights and taking out bags I couldn't see through. I wondered if they were taking all my paints and brushes. What about the mural? Had it been damaged when Bogie threw his temper tantrum?

Leo was already gone. He'd been taken into custody almost immediately. The police photographer had taken what felt like a hundred pictures of me as the EMTs stood by. Then the police left me alone and let the EMTs work.

And Detective Lee hovered.

They bandaged my lip and checked out my eyes and did all the routine stuff that I guess happens after someone beats you up pretty thoroughly without doing any serious damage. According to them, I'd have a lot of bruises and I had a nasty cut lip, but other than that, I was fine.

Of course, I wouldn't have been fine if Leo had managed to dose me with the lethal syringe of heroine he'd had in his pocket. They found that on the floor among all the boxes that Bogie had somehow, miraculously, managed to throw at Leo. Bogie had disappeared. I couldn't even feel him around me as Detective Lee hovered. Whatever energy he'd used had wiped him out. Vincent was around but hovering in the background, polite enough to leave me alone while I was being checked out.

"Should I call your grandmother or your mom?" Detective Lee asked.

"Neither, please." I hopped down from the back of the ambulance. "I can walk home from here."

"Walk? You must be joking."

"Chris, it's like three blocks. Please don't get weird about this, okay?"

He looked around, but only the EMT was looking at us. And yeah, she was smirking.

"Fine." He cleared his throat. "Let me tell my partner and I'll walk you home." He shoved his hands in his pockets and walked back to one of the patrol cars where a guy in a suit was talking with someone in uniform. Detective Lee spoke to him, and the other suit glanced at me, nodded, and continued talking to the uniform.

He waited for me to grab my bag and thank the EMT, then we walked down Howland Canal, leaving Leo Caralt's house behind us. We got away from the lights and the foot traffic, nearly to Ocean Avenue, before Detective Lee pulled me behind a giant oleander bush and wrapped me in a fierce hug.

"Dammit, Linx. I'm so pissed at you right now."

I let myself relax against his chest. I lifted my arms and slid them around his waist, bringing him closer. He squeezed me tightly, and for the first time that night, I felt the shock start to set in. I began to shiver as he made soothing sounds and rubbed my back. I didn't cry. Not quite. But there were tears in my eyes. I felt… fragile. That's what it was. I felt like I might break apart if he didn't keep holding me together. He rocked me back and forth in his arms. I'm pretty sure he kissed the top of my head, but I can't put money on that.

"When you sent that text, I nearly jumped out of my skin," he said. "I don't even know what I yelled at Marquez when I got him on the phone."

"I'm sorry."

"Fucking hell, Linx." His words were angry, but his tone was relieved. "That could have been really bad."

"I know."

"What were you thinking?"

Bogie would have said, Not much. I chose to remain

silent. I'd been thinking I was angry and sick of putting up with Leo. Clearly that was not the most mature attitude to have.

"Next time I'll definitely come up with a better plan," I said quietly.

"Next time?" He pulled back. "Are you kidding me?"

I chose to go the wide-eyed and silent route.

"There is no next time, Linx." Detective Lee—Chris —unzipped his hoodie and wrapped it around me, helping me put it on as I winced. My shoulder was going to be pretty sore. Then he tucked me under his arm and started walking to my grandmother's house. "Next time…," he muttered again.

"Thanks for saving my life so quickly."

"You're welcome. Don't break into any more murderers' houses and we'll call it even."

"You know, I wasn't certain he was the killer. It was more of an educated guess."

"Are you ever going to tell me everything?"

I looked up at him. "Would you believe me?"

He shook his head and kept walking.

"So the syringe of heroine, that's going to be enough, right?"

"That and your testimony about Caralt saying he killed them. If we're really lucky, he'll confess."

"I don't see that happening." Leo was too egotistical for that, and he'd likely get a very, very high-priced lawyer. Which meant I was going to have to testify. Which meant I was going to have to be creative about how I knew Vincent because that was sure to come out. "Maybe he'll confess."

A girl could dream, right?

"Depending on what we find when we search his stuff, you may not need to be involved. I think we're going to have a strong case, even without his attack on you. If nothing else, just the pictures from tonight paint a pretty grim picture." He paused and I stopped next to him. "What happened in that office, Linx? I've been in there before. Every single box was off the shelves, even the ones on the top. There was no ladder. Nothing that could reach all the way up there."

I bit my lip. "Someone got angry."

Disbelief warred with trust in his eyes. "Someone who could reach the top shelves?"

"Yeah."

He opened his mouth. Closed it.

Then we kept walking home.

———

I SAT on the edge of my bed, staring at the list Vincent and I had worked up. I was on it. So was Raul. Other than that, there were only about a dozen names.

"Are you sure?" I asked him.

He shrugged. "I lost touch with a lot of my college friends. These are the ones who'll show up and be nice to my parents."

I nodded. "The police already talked to her."

"Did they downplay the theft?"

My face must not have been reassuring. "Hey," I said

as he grimaced, "they still love you. Stealing some comics and a baseball card from a rich guy doesn't mean you deserved to die."

"I just wish…" He smiled sadly. "I wish I'd made better choices. I wish they could be proud of me."

"I know." This was the crappy part of being a medium. This was the part my mom dealt with far more than I ever had to.

Regret.

I never want to regret anything in life. I never want to wait to do something important or take part in anything I know would embarrass my mom or grandmother. Why?

Because I know how short life can be.

Vincent didn't start out a thief. And he didn't plan to end as one. For him, it was a means to an end. Some quick money for not much work. Hell, he might have even had noble intentions at one point. Rob from the rich and give to the poor or something.

But life doesn't work that way, and fate is a fickle thing. You don't get to explain yourself after you're dead. All you have then is the people you helped and the people you hurt.

Vincent wasn't a bad guy, but he hurt people. He'd done things that would haunt his parents forever.

He asked, "Can you take the list to my mom?"

I nodded. It was the least I could do after I'd lied to her. No doubt she'd ask me if I knew about the theft. I had already decided I'd say no. Let Vincent's mom think it was one stupid mistake and he wasn't like that. It was a lie, but a lie I could live with.

I drove to Vincent's house and suffered through an awkward cup of tea with his crushed mom. I gave her the list of his friends with their phone numbers and told her to call me when things for the funeral were arranged. I offered to help, but her sister was still there. She had help.

It was awful.

I sat in my car afterward with tears in my eyes, sad and angry at the same time. Bogie still hadn't shown up, and it had been almost a week. All I had was Vincent with me.

Vincent was not Bogie.

"I'm sorry," he said. "I'm sorry I put you through all this. I'm sorry you got hurt by Leo. But I'm really glad you helped the police solve our murders."

I nodded.

"I think…" He was gazing at the house. "I think I'm going to stay here. Just for a little while. I think I can do that now."

A weight lifted from me. "Yeah?"

He disappeared and reappeared on the other side of the car, standing outside the driver's side window. He was wearing a small smile and a black Paramore hoodie. "Yeah, I think I'll stay here."

I nodded. "Don't stay too long, okay?"

"Okay."

"When you see the light, it's time to go."

That much my mom and gran had told me. It was normal for spirits to hang around loved ones for a little while, but if they hung around too long, it made it difficult for the living to move on. Vincent wouldn't do his mom or dad any favors by staying too long.

But for a little while, it was okay.

He turned to me. "Take care of yourself, okay?"

"I will."

"You should listen to Bogie. He really cares about you, you know?"

I smiled. "Thanks, Vincent."

He walked across the street and was gone.

I didn't see him again.

I WOKE up at three in the morning to the smell of cigarette smoke in the air. I looked around, but I couldn't see anything. Then, from the corner of my eye, I saw the faint edge of a fedora. I smiled.

"Hey, Frank."

Hey, kid. His voice was just a whisper in my head.

"I didn't get the chance to say thank you before you disappeared."

I know. People have shit manners these days.

"Bitch, bitch, bitch." I rolled over and closed my eyes. "Welcome back."

In my mind, I heard the faint sound of Frank Sinatra singing "I'll Be Seeing You."

And then, with Frank back safe and sound, I slept easy for the first time in a week.

Epilogue: I'll Be Seeing You

"PAGE."

Glancing sideways, I reached over and turned the sports page for Bogie. It was Saturday morning and the coffee was on. My mom was weeding in the garden, and my nan was humming by the stove. She was chipper. Unusually chipper.

Hmmm.

"Lindsay, is Frank feeling back to his old self again?"

"I am, Peggy. Thanks for asking."

"He says he's fine." It had been two weeks since "the incident." I referred to it as the incident. Mom and Nan referred to it as "Lindsay's idiocy."

I felt so loved.

Leo Caralt was in jail because the judge had denied bail based on his status as a flight risk. I guess he owned a bunch of houses in foreign countries and they could also prove he had foreign bank accounts, so they didn't trust him not to run from the double murder charge.

I was probably going to testify unless they worked out a deal.

Vincent hadn't shown up again. His memorial service had taken place a week after the incident, and I hadn't felt his presence. I was hoping that meant he'd already moved on. My mom went with me and didn't sense him around his parents, so that made me feel better.

Bogie was... Bogie. Back to his usual cantankerous, judgmental self. Frank was bitching about the Dodgers and complaining about my hair, which I'd decided to dye a vivid bluish green to take my mind off almost being murdered. Raul approved. Frank did not.

Raul was also back to normal. He'd kept his distance until he and his boyfriend had gotten into a rip-roaring fight about Raul meeting the boyfriend's family. After that he'd called me to yell about "Dominic facing reality," and we'd gabbed about the fickleness of men for an hour. Halfway through the conversation, Raul had mumbled something about missing me and I'd mumbled something back.

Then we'd quickly moved on. We weren't the best about confronting the past.

So everything was back to normal! I should have been happy. I mostly was. I'd gotten a call from a local restaurant about doing a new mural for their roof balcony, and the job was supposed to start at the end of the month.

I was working.

My family was fine.

Bogie was back.

Raul was speaking to me again.

Leo Caralt was going to prison (probably).

And... Chris Lee hadn't called me or texted since the incident.

Okay, fine. I was moping about it. In fact, my mom had snapped at me this morning to get out of my head and "Just call the man already. Are you fifteen?"

Call me crazy (trust me, you wouldn't be the first) but I wanted him to make the first move. I'd laid myself bare during the investigation and confessed all my weirdness. The man hadn't responded in kind. He'd been the hero and walked me home and kissed the top of my head (I think) and given me the mother of all manly hugs.

Then... nothing.

Nothing!

"Page!"

"Stop shouting." I glared at Bogie.

"I said page five times. Where is your brain? Did it run screaming from the candy-colored crap on your head?"

I turned to him and blew the scent of coffee in his face before I took a long drink. "Mmmmm. Coffee. Perfect, hot coffee. Freshly brewed."

Frank turned back to the sport section. "You know, you say you're a modern gal, but you're letting this one take the reins. Not very feminist of you."

"I'm not taking dating advice from a guy who's been dead for over sixty years."

"You should."

"Shut up."

The doorbell rang.

"Oh!" My nan turned from the stove and turned the burner off under the eggs she'd been scrambling. "I wonder who that could be."

"From the look on your face, you already know," I said. "Is it Mrs. L.?"

Mrs. Lamberti hadn't returned to her house yet. She was still visiting her son in Colorado. Part of me was wondering if she might be staying.

Nan walked out of the kitchen and down the hall. I heard the door open and a few mumbled words, but whoever was at the door didn't speak very loudly.

The footsteps coming down the hall sounded male though. I turned, expecting Raul.

It was not Raul.

I sat silent as Detective Christopher Lee sat across from me, wearing a crisp grey suit and a blue tie. He set his sunglasses and keys on the table as Nan brought him a cup of coffee.

"Thanks, Mrs. Maxwell."

"Peggy, Detective. I told you."

"I'll try to remember." He smiled at my grand-mother before he looked at me. "Morning, Linx."

Of course I was wearing my ratty pajama shorts and a Han Solo shirt that said I'm Nice Men. Of course I was.

"Hi," I said. "So… what's going on here?"

"Peggy invited me for breakfast."

"Did she?"

A smile was threatening the corner of his mouth. "She did."

"Interesting."

"I guess she didn't tell you, huh?"

"Nope." I took a long drink of coffee. Shit shit shit. My head was spinning.

Bogie said, "Good call, Peggy. She wasn't going to get off her ass anytime soon."

I ignored both Bogie and my nan, who was extra-super chipper as she served Chris a plate of scrambled eggs and toast to go with his coffee.

"Thanks, Peggy. It looks delicious."

"Are you working all weekend, Detective?"

"You better call me Chris if I'm calling you Peggy," he said. "And yes. It's my turn." He turned to look at me. "I was at that conference last week in Reno. Just got back into town. Not that anyone here would know that."

I bit into a piece of toast. "Hmm." Swallowed. "Is my grandma supposed to keep track of your work schedule?"

"I wouldn't expect her to. I was just... informing."

Informing what? Me that he'd been out of town working? Was that supposed to explain why I hadn't heard from him?

"I've been busy too," I said. "Really busy."

"With what?"

Uh... dying my hair? Cleaning the garage so I could use it as a studio? (Okay, I cleared a path, let's not get crazy.)

I swallowed another gulp of coffee. "Artist stuff."

"Artist stuff? Is that a technical term?"

"Yes."

"I like the hair."

Nan said, "I'm going to call your mother in from the garden. These eggs will get cold if she doesn't come to eat."

I set my coffee down as soon as she walked out the french doors. "Bogie, out."

"You expect me to just—"

"Out!"

I didn't care how crazy it made me look. To his credit, Chris didn't blink when I talked to thin air.

"Fine," Bogie muttered. "Don't mess this up, kid."

I kept my eyes on Christopher Lee, homicide detective not scared away by the house full of crazy women. "What are you doing here?"

"I told you—"

"No, *what* are you doing here?"

He leaned forward. "Why didn't you text me?"

"Why didn't you text me?"

"Because it's complicated, Linx. You're a witness. I'm a detective. You're a…"

"Psychic?"

"I believe medium would be more accurate according to what you've told me."

Sitting there, cool as you please. He was talking about mediums and psychics like he was taking notes in his little notebook. He wasn't even using the crazy-person voice.

Chris glanced around the room. "Is there…?"

"Anyone here? No. Not right now."

"But there was."

"Yeah, there was. There's one ghost in particular who likes to hang around. He's a detective like you."

"Not like me," Chris said. "I'm not invisible."

No, he was not. He was just as handsome as the day I met him. And he smelled even better.

"Not like you." I wasn't attracted to Bogie. Not in the least. Christopher Lee, on the other hand… "What are you doing here?" I asked in a smaller voice.

Chris leaned back, still staring at me. The corner of his mouth turned up. He looked around my nan's crazy kitchen decorated with too many coffee cups and vintage postcards glued to the wall. To the empty chair beside me and the sports page lying open. Then he picked up his fork and dug into his eggs.

"I'm having breakfast," he said. "You should get some. It's not good to have coffee on an empty stomach."

Who was this man? I stood and walked to the stove to serve myself. I scooped some eggs from the pan and refilled my coffee.

"I like the shirt," Chris said. "Have you seen the new movie yet?"

"No. I have mixed feelings."

"I hear it's better than people expected."

"Good to know." I sat down across from him. That little smile was still at the corner of his mouth. "Detective Lee?"

He smiled. "Yes?"

"What are we doing here?"

"Having breakfast." He sipped his coffee.

"Okay." I picked up my fork. Set it down. "So… what? This is a thing we do now? You come over to my house and have breakfast on Saturday morning?"

"Yes." He picked up his knife and buttered the toast Nan had given him. "This is a thing we do now."

"Do I have a say in it?"

He looked me straight in the eye. "Always."

I had nothing to say to that. I picked up my fork and started eating. He was right. The eggs were really good.

"Okay," I said. "This is a thing we do now."

He looked up at me and our eyes met. The moment held and stretched like a drop of paint clinging to a brush.

I know you, that look said. *I see you.*

The tension broke when my nan and mother came back through the french doors, chatting about the whole bus of tourists that had just unloaded right off Sherman Canal.

"I don't think it should be legal for those big tour buses to park there," Nan said. "Is it legal, Chris?"

"It's legal."

"But is it ethical?" my mother asked. "I mean, this is a neighborhood. Do they bother the people in Beverly Hills like this? No, because they have money to keep people out."

"Technically, they can't keep people out of Beverly Hills either," Chris said. "And we can't cite tour operators for being unethical."

"You should be able to," Mom said. "Don't you think, Lindsay?"

I stuffed toast in my mouth and said, "Mmflnmmr."

Chris had dimples. And twinkly eyes. That just wasn't fair. There needed to be some check on his attractiveness. He was bordering on unethical simply by existing.

"Oh," he said. "Did you see this?" He pulled a folded piece of newspaper from his jacket pocket. "I'm looking for a new place, and it was in the real estate section."

"You're looking for a new place?"

He shrugged and spread out the newspaper section. "Yeah."

"In Venice?"

"If I can afford it." He pointed at a column. "Look."

New listing. By appointment only. Modern and newly renovated house in a coveted location on Howland Canal. Three bedrooms and three bathrooms. Roof deck. Modern security system and soundproofing. Office features a custom mural by celebrated urban artist, Linx Maxwell.

Celebrated urban artist...

I looked up at Chris and my smile was in danger of breaking my face. "Seriously?"

He nodded. "Seriously."

"Seriously!" The smile fell. "You're not thinking of buying that house, are you?"

"On my salary? Are you kidding?"

"Oh, thank God."

"Good to know the poverty of your public servants doesn't concern you."

"Nope." I turned and shoved the clipping in my mother's face. "Look at this! Mom, look! The paper called me a celebrated urban artist! Look, Creepy Leo's house is on the market and the mural is a selling point!"

As soon as my mother saw it, she squealed like a

seven-year-old at a birthday party. There was much cele-
bration, and I didn't care if I looked cool in front of
Chris or not. Nan immediately suggested mimosas, even
though Chris had to decline.

Celebrated urban artist.

Chris raised his coffee cup when we toasted, and
from the corner of my eye, I saw Bogie leaning against
the wall, his fedora tilted forward and a wry smile on
his face.

Way to go, kid.

Nan was telling Chris about some of my worst
artistic flubs as a kid while Mom was dialing Raul, probably to invite him over to have breakfast with the "celebrated urban artist."

I'm proud of you, Linx.

Before he disappeared, I turned to Bogie and
winked. He tapped the brim of his hat and faded into
the wall.

He'd be back. But this moment…

This moment was for the living.

THE END

Sign up for a free short story

Thank you for taking the time to read this book! If you enjoy a book, one of the best things you can do to support an author is to leave an honest review wherever you bought your copy. Thank you for taking the time to let others know what you thought.

Sign up for my newsletter today and receive a bonus short story "Too Many Cooks" FREE in your inbox! Subscribers receive monthly updates, new book alerts, exclusive contests, and original short fiction featuring favorite characters from my books.

Preview: INK

Please enjoy this preview of INK, book one in Elizabeth Hunter's new contemporary romance series, Love Stories on Seventh and Main.

———

Emmie Elliot lasted three breaths in the old bookshop, her measured exhalations stirring dust motes that danced in the afternoon light streaming in from the large display windows that looked over Main Street. She backed out the front door and turned her back on Metlin Books, staring at the lazy midday traffic driving south on 7th Avenue. Then she bent over, braced her hands on her knees, and let her auburn hair fall, shielding her face from the afternoon sun.

Daisy walked out of the corner shop and came to stand beside her. "What's going on? You're even paler than usual."

"I can't do it."

"Can't do what?"

Emmie straightened. "I can't sell the shop."

Daisy's eyes went wide. "I thought you and your gran—"

"Yeah." Emmie took a deep breath, clearing the dust from her lungs. "I know."

What are you doing, Emmie?

She had no idea.

She'd spent her whole life trying to get away from this town. The bookstore was her grandmother's. Sure, she'd grown up in it, and sure, she worked in a bookstore in San Francisco, but that was just temporary. She was just doing that until something happened. Something bigger. More important. More… something.

Emmie was twenty-seven and still waiting for something big to happen. She had a job she tolerated, an apartment she loved. No husband, no boyfriend, a mother she barely spoke to. She didn't even have a cat.

Her assets in the world consisted of a newish car, a very small inheritance from her grandma Betsy, a circle of carefully chosen friends, and a three-unit retail building on the corner of Main Street and 7th Avenue, right in the heart of Metlin, a sleepy town in the middle of Central California.

She and her grandmother had talked about it a year ago, when they knew the cancer wasn't going into remission. Emmie was supposed to sell the building and use the proceeds as a nest egg for…

They'd never really talked about that part.

"What's going on, Em? What are you thinking?"

Daisy frowned and twisted a lock of dark wavy hair back in the bun on top of her head. It was afternoon, but she was still wearing her apron from baking that morning. With her tan skin, dark eyes, and retro apron, Daisy looked like an updated Latina June Cleaver if you didn't notice the tattoos at her wrists.

Her friend Tayla had offered to accompany her from San Francisco, but Emmie had refused. Emmie was taking a full two weeks off work from Bay City Books, but Tayla worked at a big accounting firm and couldn't afford to take the time off. She'd never been to Metlin and had no desire to visit. Tayla was a city girl to her bones.

It's fine, Emmie had told her. *It's not like I have any reason to stay. My mom cleaned out my grandma's apartment. I'll visit Daisy and Spider, sign papers to put the place on the market, and leave.*

Emmie straightened her button-down blouse and played with the buttons on the sleeve of her cardigan. She wasn't dressed for Metlin; she was dressed for an upscale bookshop in Union Square. If anyone from her childhood were to pass by, they would have a hard time putting Emmie's sleek hair and tidy, professional appearance together with the rumpled girl who'd spent most of her life hiding behind a book.

She didn't belong in Metlin anymore. She never had. She'd always wanted a bigger life. A more important life around people who liked music and art and travel, not farmers and mechanics and ranchers.

Daisy said, "I know you must have sentimental

attachment to the building, but I'm not sure you realize—"

"How bad it was?" Emmie picked at a thread on one of her buttons, twisting it between her thumb and forefinger. "I know how bad it was. Grandma was completely up-front with me."

Emmie had no illusions about the state of Metlin Books. The shop was barely hanging on. The only thing her grandma'd had going for her was that she owned the building, the apartment above it, and rented to two successful neighbors, a family hardware business and Café Maya, Daisy's restaurant.

She walked over and sat on the cast-iron bench in front of the bookstore windows, kicking at the doggie water dish chained to the bench. The dish that had remained dry since her grandmother had passed six months before. "Bookstores are not a good bet."

"Not generally, no."

"She told me not to be noble." Emmie eyed the water dish again. Then she took the water bottle out of her purse and dumped the contents in the bowl. "We had a plan. Sell the shop with provisions for you and Ethan—"

"Leave me and Ethan out of it," Daisy said. "I loved your grandma, but I think I can speak for Ethan—"

"Speak for me how?" Ethan Vasquez, owner of Main Street Hardware, set down the A-frame sign advertising daily deals and walked toward Daisy and Emmie. "Em, you all right?"

Daisy kept talking. "We both loved Betsy, but this is your life and inheritance, so don't worry about us."

"What's going on?" Ethan and Daisy hovered over her.

Daisy straightened. "Emmie's not sure about selling the shop."

"Great!"

"No," Daisy said. "Not great. This was not the plan."

And all of Emmie's friends knew how much Emmie liked a plan. She was famous for them. Emmie would plan a night out three days in advance and email a detailed schedule to everyone "so they were on the same page." She didn't do spontaneous. The idea of returning to Metlin permanently was giving her heart palpitations.

You're waiting, a little voice in her head whispered. *What are you waiting for?*

Ethan crossed his arms over his barrel chest and let out a long breath. "You know I can't be unbiased on this one."

"So stay out of it."

"I *am* staying out of it." He scratched his beard thoughtfully. "That's why I'm reminding her I can't be unbiased."

Emmie looked up and took a deep breath. "Don't be unbiased. I want your opinion."

"A new owner is likely to kick me and Dad out," he said. "Just when I'm turning things around. You know that. Our shop is huge, and space on Main Street is at a premium these days. A new owner would likely split our store in half and make double what we're paying now. So of course I want you to stay." He crouched down.

"Metlin's different, Emmie. It's not the same town you left."

"That I can agree with," Daisy said.

"And I know the store needs work," Ethan continued, "but me and my dad would help you out. Anything you need. We're free labor after all the favors Betsy did for us over the years. You know that, right?"

Ethan's big brown eyes pleaded with her. Emmie looked past him to the new paint on his store, the fresh awning, the racks of vegetable starts for backyard gardens. Main Street Hardware had been flailing until Ethan came back from college four years ago and revamped his family business.

Now, instead of depending on the dwindling business of the retirement crowd, Main Street Hardware appealed to young do-it-yourselfers in their late twenties like Ethan and his buddies who were buying the old Craftsman cottages south of downtown and fixing them up. Ethan led workshops on container gardening, and his dad taught plasterwork and hardwood-floor-refinishing courses.

Beyond the hardware store, Café Maya bustled with midday customers. It was a narrow café and bakery started by Daisy's grandmother Maya, who'd come from Oaxaca and started the restaurant with determination and a treasure trove of recipes. Daisy's mother had modernized the menu, and Daisy had added a bakery. Café Maya was a Metlin institution and business had remained solid.

Beyond Emmie's building, stretching west, sat the rest of downtown. Sitting at the base of the Sierra

Nevada mountains, Metlin had never been big enough to attract attention from any of the big chains. It had only ever had one bookstore, Metlin Books. And for as long as anyone could remember, it had been run by the Elliot family. Emmie's great-grandfather had bought the building and started a book and toy store. Eventually the toys left and her grandmother had focused on the books. Emmie's mom, despite her bookish roots, had never been a reader and lived an itinerant life as a working musician. She was happy, but Metlin wasn't her home.

But for Emmie—growing up in the fishbowl of Metlin—the bookshop had been her home, her refuge, and the gateway to a much larger world.

"I have an apartment in San Francisco," she said quietly. "Friends. A life. A job."

Ethan asked, "Aren't you working in a bookstore up there?"

"Yeah."

He frowned. "But you *own* a bookstore here. Why on earth would you live in San Francisco, pay God knows what in rent, and get paid to work at someone else's business when you could own your own business here doing exactly the same thing?"

Daisy said, "Back off."

"She knows I'm right." He stood and pointed at Emmie. "You know I'm right."

Emmie's stayed silent. She didn't deal with confrontation well, but Ethan wasn't entirely wrong. How many times had she tried to change something at the bookstore she worked at in the city, only to be told "that wasn't the way things were done" at Bay City Books?

Still, she hesitated. "I manage a store. I don't know if I could run a business. My grandma wasn't like your dad. She didn't give me a lot of responsibility in the shop. I know nothing about bookkeeping or—"

"You'd figure it out," he said. "You're one of the smartest people I know. You helped me with my place when I was drowning."

She shrugged. "You would have come up with those ideas on your own with enough time."

"I doubt it. You have a great brain for marketing. You know what people like now. How to put everything online. How to find the right customers."

Daisy shook her head. "Books are a tough business, Ethan. I know exactly how much Betsy was making with this place, and rent from your place and my café was the only thing paying her bills. Competing with online retailers—"

"Can't be any tougher than competing with the megamart hardware stores," Ethan said. "Emmie knows—"

"Emmie knows"—Emmie stood and cut them both off—"she needs to spend some time thinking about this."

Daisy's mouth fought off a smile. "Emmie also knows she needs to stop talking in third person, right? Because it's obnoxious."

"Whatever you do," Ethan said, "don't talk to Asshole Adrian until you've made up your mind."

Emmie frowned. "Adrian? Adrian from high school?"

"Yeah, Adrian Saroyan. He's in real estate now. And he's an asshole."

Daisy tried to shove Ethan away. "Ignore him. You know he never liked Adrian."

"Nobody likes Adrian." Ethan let Daisy shove him. "You were the only one who liked him, Em."

"Me and the female half of my high school class." Emmie watched Daisy—a foot shorter than Ethan—shove the big man back to his shop.

Ethan repositioned his sign. "He's a dipshit and an asshole."

Daisy said, "He stole your girlfriend; that's the only reason you hate him."

"That's not the only reason," Ethan muttered. "Just one of them."

Emmie left them bickering and walked back into the bookshop. She stood in the mosaic-tiled entryway and examined it with critical eyes.

Pros: She owned it, free and clear. It had a recognizable name and a good location. It was a beautiful space with huge built-in shelves and custom woodwork her giant bookstore in San Francisco tried to imitate but never really could. Metlin Books had history. Charm. And a two-bedroom apartment over the shop. If she lived here, she would have no commute and no rent.

Cons: Profits under her grandmother had been pretty much zero. The only real income was from renting the rest of the building, and that just paid the bills. The bookshop was a ton of work with a very small profit margin. She'd be solely responsible for it. There would be no vacation days accrued. No retirement plan. No one else paying the bills. No one to call in sick to.

But it's mine.

Yes, it was. Emmie walked around the shop, rifling through the stacks of used books her grandmother had collected. Most of the new inventory was so old she could never sell it at cover price. She'd be starting over.

Betsy had stocked lots of romances, but nothing modern. There was a nice stack of vintage Harlequins she might be able to sell online to a collector. She needed far more new names. Romance ran bookstores. She'd have to get an updated selection and figure out how to buy from self-published authors who made up so many of the new writers these days. It was something she'd pushed for at Bay City, but the owners were complete snobs about self-publishing.

The shop had a good mystery section, but it leaned toward cozies. Her grandmother hadn't cared for thrillers or any dark psychology.

Hardly any literary fiction or poetry, but in Metlin that was probably a safe call.

Nonfiction was in dire need of updating. Judging from the traffic at Ethan's store, gardening manuals and idea books would probably sell well, as would interior design and home-improvement stuff.

With growing tourist traffic from the national park, local history and outdoor guides could be a winner.

Emmie wandered across the shop and looked out the windows just as a trio of motorcycles revved their engines at the intersection of 7th and Main. Emmie watched two guys in an animated discussion in front of the custom-car-upholstery shop and listened to the buzz of music and voices from Ice House Brews that sat catty-corner to Metlin Books at the intersection. Directly across from her on Main was Bombshell Tattoos. Beyond it, a specialty cigar and smoking club. A couple with vividly dyed hair and heavy ink left the tattoo shop hand in hand and walked past the T-shirt shop on Main headed toward Top Shelf Comics and Games.

What books would that couple read? How about the guys in front of the car shop? Graphic novels? Steam-punk? Auto history?

Emmie watched from behind her windows as a trio of women dragged a giant mirror from one of the antique shops farther down 7th, laughing as they tried to fit it in the back of a battered pickup truck. Decorating books. DIY manuals.

Across the street, a graffiti-style mural decorated the front of an art-supply store next to an auto-body shop. Art history books? Political science?

Ethan was right. Metlin was changing. The indus-trial and the traditional were colliding and creating something odd and new and more than a little cool. And Emmie realized the bookshop—her bookshop—was sitting right in the middle of it all.

Maybe she hadn't belonged in the old Metlin, but times changed. Towns changed. People changed.

This was not in the plan, her logical side said.

Maybe the plan needs to change.

Emmie pulled out her phone. Her finger shook as

she touched Tayla's number and waited for her best friend to pick up.

"Hey!" she answered. "Did you get everything signed? How's Daisy?"

Emmie took a deep breath, stirring the dust again. "I have an idea. And it might be crazy or it might be amazing."

"If it's a really good idea, it'll be both. And it might also involve handcuffs or Silly String."

She blinked. "Silly String?"

"Do you really want to know? You sound weird."

"I didn't sign any papers to sell the shop."

"Okay…?"

"I think you should quit your job, move down to Metlin with me, and help me reopen the bookshop."

Tayla didn't say a word.

Emmie squeezed her eyes shut. "I know it sounds nuts, but you can have free rent."

Her best friend remained silent.

"Tayla, please say something."

"Maybe it's because I caught one of the senior partners staring at my boobs *again* today, but I am actually considering this."

Emmie tried not to jump up and down with excitement.

"That's not a yes. Or a no," Tayla said. "But… maybe?"

"I'll take maybe."

"Tell you what, it's Friday. I'll catch the train tomorrow morning," Tayla said. "I can't guarantee anything, but I want to see this hick town you claim to hate but now suddenly want me to move to."

"I'll meet you at the station."

"Is this a result of valley fever?" Tayla asked. "I've read about that, you know."

"I don't have valley fever."

"Isn't that something someone with valley fever would say?"

Emmie squeezed her eyes shut. "Tayla, I can't explain it. I just think it might be awesome. Or nuts. But you know how you were getting on my case last month for always being cautious and never taking chances?"

"Yep."

"This…" Emmie turned around in the empty shop. "This is a chance."

———

INK is available now
at all major retailers.

Acknowledgments

This has been such a weird and wonderful season of life. I want to thank my readers for their patience and enthusiasm for this story and all my work! I hope you've enjoyed the newest installment of Linx and her ghost. There will be more to come!

Super-extreme-profuse thanks to Jenn Beach, my assistant, who has kept life on an even keel for me the past few months. More super-extreme-profuse thanks to Gen, my assister extraordinaire.

Thanks to my editing team over at Victory Editing. Anne and Linda are the pros who make me look good. And many, many thanks to the awesome creators at Damonza who capture the fun and mystery of this series with their excellent covers.

And finally, thanks to my amazing family! I love you all so much.

About the Author

ELIZABETH HUNTER is a *USA Today* and international best-selling author of romance, contemporary fantasy, and paranormal mystery. Based in Central California, she travels extensively to write fantasy fiction exploring world mythologies, history, and the universal bonds of love, friendship, and family. She has published over thirty works of fiction and sold over a million books worldwide. She is the author of Love Stories on 7th and Main, the Elemental Legacy series, the Irin Chronicles, the Cambio Springs Mysteries, and other works of fiction.

Also by Elizabeth Hunter

Contemporary Romance

The Genius and the Muse

7th and Main

INK

HOOKED (Winter 2019)

Linx & Bogie

A Ghost in the Glamour

A Bogie in the Boat

The Cambio Springs Series

Long Ride Home (short story)

Shifting Dreams

Five Mornings (short story)

Desert Bound

Waking Hearts

The Irin Chronicles

The Scribe

The Singer

The Secret

The Staff and the Blade

The Silent

The Storm

The Seeker (Fall 2018)

The Elemental Mysteries

A Hidden Fire

This Same Earth

The Force of Wind

A Fall of Water

The Elemental World

Building From Ashes

Waterlocked (novella)

Blood and Sand

The Bronze Blade (novella)

The Scarlet Deep

Beneath a Waning Moon (novella)

A Stone-Kissed Sea

The Elemental Legacy

Shadows and Gold

Imitation and Alchemy

Omens and Artifacts

Midnight Labyrinth

Blood Apprentice (Winter 2018)

Made in the USA
Lexington, KY
22 September 2018